Adam grinned. 'I'm terribly flattered that you want to be alone with me,' he murmured. 'Shall I kiss you now, or may I drink my coffee first?'

Sara's jaw dropped. 'I don't——That wasn't what I had in mind at all!'

His eyes were warmly appreciative as his gaze skimmed over her body. And even though he hadn't touched her, she found herself tingling from head to foot as if every square inch of her skin were being caressed by a lover's hand.

That's impossible, she thought. I stopped feeling those things years ago. And I don't plan to get caught in that trap ever again.

LET ME COUNT THE WAYS

BY

LEIGH MICHAELS

MILLS & BOON LIMITED
ETON HOUSE   18-24 PARADISE ROAD
RICHMOND   SURREY   TW9 1SR

First published in Great Britain 1988
by Mills & Boon Limited

© Leigh Michaels 1988

Australian copyright 1988
Philippine copyright 1989
This edition 1989

ISBN 0 263 76196 7

Set in Palacio 10 on 11 pt.
01 – 8901 – 57812

Typeset in Great Britain by JCL Graphics, Bristol

Made and printed in Great Britain

CHAPTER ONE

SHE had skipped lunch and worked straight through, but by mid-afternoon Sara Prentiss was willing to admit that perhaps she had bitten off a little more work then she should have attempted. Chandler College's summer session classes would start the day after tomorrow, and, the way it looked, she wasn't going to be able to find her way out of her office by then, much less have it back in order.

She sat down on a pile of books, because her chair was loaded with manilla folders from the top drawer of her filing cabinet, and studied the mess. The problem, she told herself, was that one task always led to another. She hadn't really intended to take every book off the shelves, for example. She was only going to sort out the ones that she no longer used on a regular basis and box them up for long-term storage or to send over to the library. But then she had realised that the whole office would be more efficent if the adjustable shelves were rearranged, and so, in a grand burst of enthusiasm, at eight o'clock this morning, when she had been fresh and energetic——

'Fresh, heck,' Sara muttered. 'I couldn't even comprehend what I was doing. I was still bleary-eyed at that hour.'

And as a result it was now mid-afternoon and here she was with her office looking like a frontier fort, with textbooks instead of logs forming the palisade.

She wearily pushed herself up off the stack of books and wiped her damp palms on the seat of her jeans. It was hot, too—this end of the campus was almost deserted, and the air-conditioning wouldn't be turned on in the liberal arts building until the day classes started. Sara looked longingly out the window and across the car park to the old building, where her office had been last summer. The floors weren't level and the stairs creaked and the radiators rattled, but there had been one good thing about the old liberal arts building—the window would open to let in the softness of a summer breeze flowing off the river.

But that's progress, Sara thought, and Chandler College had made plenty of progress in the last few years. It seemed that there wasn't an area of the campus that was safe to walk across because of all the construction that was going on, especially since the new president had take over. But it wasn't only new buildings that Dave Talbot had brought to the campus; his enthusiastic ideas sometimes threatened to shake Chandler to its conservative roots. Sara sighed at the thought of his latest brilliant idea . . .

She found a rubber band in her desk drawer and pulled her honey-coloured hair up off her neck and into an untidy ponytail. Then, with dogged determination rather than enthusiasm, she went back to work.

Most of the books were dusted and back on the shelves, and she was starting to sort out the flotsam of an entire academic year from her files, when the sound of footsteps in the hall startled her. Strange that anyone would be coming in so late, she thought. It was almost five o'clock.

She was hearing more than one set of footsteps, she realised. Then a masculine voice said, 'We've assigned you this office on a temporary basis. I'm sorry you'll have to share; even with the new building, we're still short of space. But Professor Ryan is only teaching one class this summer, so he won't be around much. If there is anything you need——'

She recognised the voice; the head of the English department was just down the hall. Nothing short of emergency would take Hal Mitchell away from his research on a day when students weren't on campus to interrupt, and that could only mean that the man with him, the second set of footsteps, was the bigwig Dave Talbot had talked into spending the summer teaching at Chandler. The bigwig who wasn't supposed to arrive until tomorrow——

'Damn,' Sara said under her breath. She took one comprehensive look at the mess and gave her office door a gentle push, hoping that it would slip shut silently enough so that Hal Mitchell wouldn't notice she was there. Instead, it stopped half-way.

Darned new buildings, she thought. Over in the old one, she'd had to keep a rock handy to prop her door open!

'I see Dr Prentiss is in her office,' Hal Mitchell said. 'Let me introduce you.'

An instant later two men appeared in the half-open door. Hal looked around vaguely and said, 'Oh, good. I'm glad you've got everything in order, Sara, before classes start.'

She could see, from the corner of her eye, the other man's eyebrows raise as if he wanted to say, *This is in order?*, and she started to seethe. Hal Mitchell was a dear, she thought, and there was nothing he didn't know about the Shakespearean era, but when it came to modern living he always seemed to view things through a piece of gauze . . .

'I'm working on it, Hal,' she said smoothly, and turned to the other man with her hand outstretched. 'You must be Adam Merrill.' Carry it off like a professional, Sara, she ordered herself. Pretend it doesn't bother you to have a celebrity walk into your office when it looks like this, and it won't matter at all.

And the man was a genuine celebrity, she had to admit. Even though Sara happened to think that his work was trash of the worst kind, lots of people disagreed—enough of them to put Adam Merrill's books on the *New York Times* bestseller list regularly, and for lengthy periods of time. Her housemate, Olivia, was one of them, and in the last year Sara had heard enough about Adam Merrill to make her thoroughly sick of the subject. But she respected Olivia's age, if not her taste in literature, and so she had developed the knack of appearing to listen attentively while thinking about something else.

The first good look Sara got jolted her. He's far better-looking than the picture on his books, she thought. His hair was almost black, and it was a little longer than most men were wearing it this year. He had a classical nose, and a strong chin with a tiny cleft in it. But it was his eyes that really startled Sara. They were the most unusual shade of violet-blue that she had ever seen, and she found herself staring, thinking, Olivia is going to be knocked off her feet. One look at him and she's going to swoon . . .

'Sara is the assistant head of the department,' Hal Mitchell was explaining. 'As I started to say before, Adam, if there is anything you need, Sara is the one to ask about it.'

'You're very young for that position, Sara,' Adam Merrill observed.

'I'm old enough, I assure you——' Sara hesitated, then said firmly, 'Adam.' If he could use first names, so could she; she was certainly no awestruck member of his fan club. She realised belatedly that he was looking a bit amused, and he was still holding her hand. She retrieved it and told herself firmly that the strange colour of his eyes was probably due to contact lenses rather than nature, anyway, and so there was no point in drooling about it.

'Sara will also be supervising your creative-writing class,' Hal Mitchell went on.

The amusement in Adam Merrill's eyes vanished. 'I understood that I was to be independent in the classroom,' he said. 'Dave Talbot assured me that what I did was completely——'

Hal Mitchell nodded. 'Of course, of course,' he said reassuringly. 'It's just a formality, really. You have all the expertise in the field that anyone could ask for, but you don't have the academic qualifications that our board of regents insists on. So officially it's listed as Dr Prentiss's class, with you assisting. Actually——'

'I see.' But Adam Merrill didn't sound very happy about it, Sara thought. His dark eyebrows had drawn together, and he was staring at her warily.

It irritated her. Who did he think he was, anyway? she wondered. 'Actually,' she pointed out, 'it was scheduled to be my creative-writing class, long before you and President Talbot decided you were coming here this summer.'

'And you're offended that I've taken it away from you?'

'You haven't,' she said crisply. 'Remember? I'm still supervising.'

'She's glad to get rid of it,' Hal Mitchell said. 'Be

honest, Sara—you hate early-morning classes, no matter what they are.' He pulled out his gold pocket-watch. 'Goodness, talking of President Talbot reminds me that we need to be getting back to his office. Sara, is there anything else Adam should know?'

Sara reached under a stack of folders on the corner of her desk and unearthed a dark red book with a title stamped on it in gold. 'Here's the textbook we use. I'm sure you'd like to familiarise yourself with it before the first class.'

'The textbook,' Adam Merrill said. It wasn't a question. He took the book, looked down at it quizzically, and added, 'And it's called *Creative Writing*. What a very—*creative* name.'

Sara found herself flushing in resentment at the irony in his tone. 'It's an excellent book. I'm sure if you'll take the trouble to look at it——'

'Oh, I will.'

'And here is the outline for the course,' she said. 'The times for the class meetings, the reading assignments, the exam schedule——'

He looked at her oddly, but he took the sheet of paper meekly and without a word followed Hal Mitchell down the hall.

She sank back in her chair and started sorting again. Paper could build up so fast, she thought. It was incredible the amount of it that could collect in a single year.

But she found her mind drifting away from the old essays she was discarding, back to the look in Adam Merrill's eyes as he had examined the outline of the course. He ought to appreciate all the work I've gone to, Sara thought. He's never taught a class like that before—he's got no idea how much organisation it takes.

Well, he soon would, she thought. Twenty-five of Chandler's best and most challenging students had signed up for that seminar. Before the five-week summer session was over, Adam Merrill would know what it was like to drown in paper . . .

If Mr Merrill thinks teaching is so easy, she thought, he'll soon find out what it's really like.

It had been such a beautiful morning that she had walked the few blocks to her office, rather than take her car out. As she walked back home, she regretted that decision, because she was tired out and depressed about the mess that still remained on her desk. It would take most of tomorrow to get it cleared up, and even that might be too optimistic an estimate if she had a lot of students dropping in to talk about their problems.

Then Phillip Reynolds called to her from the sheltered front entrance of the main administration building, and Sara regretted even more her decision to walk. If there was one thing she was simply not up to coping with this afternoon, it was Phillip.

She waved and kept walking, but he galloped across the centre of a freshly seeded patch of lawn and pulled up beside her, out of breath, with his hair standing on end and his tie flying over one shoulder.

'Lucky for you the lawns-and-gardens people didn't see you,' Sara said. 'They're a little touchy about the new grass.'

'It's the wrong time of the year to plant grass seed, anyway.' He patted himself back together. 'I need to talk to you about Olivia.'

Sara sighed. 'Is there anything new in this discussion, or is this just a reprise of the previous four hundred and twelve times you've talked to me about Olivia?'

'You know she can't keep living in that mausoleum of a house by herself.'

Sara didn't stop walking. 'She's not,' she said crisply. 'I'm living there with her.'

'But how much of the time are you there? She could fall and break a bone and lie there for hours——

'Phillip, the housekeeper is there all day; I'm there all night. There are a few hours when she's alone, but she is an adult in excellent health for her age, after all——'

'The woman's got to be at least seventy-eight, Sara, and she could get sick any minute.'

Sara bit her tongue. She happened to know that Olivia had turned eighty-two on her last birthday, but she thought that if Olivia wanted Phillip to know that, she would have told him herself. 'What are you suggesting, Phillip?'

'That she do the sensible thing. Move into one of the new apartments in that supervised-living complex across town, where there are nurses on call every minute, and——'

'And give up her independence? Worse yet, give up Ashton Court? Be reasonable, Phillip—it's her home. It's been her home for fifty-odd years. She's not an invalid, and she won't thank you for trying to make her into one.'

'Well, then, she should be more reasonable about letting me help her.'

Sara stopped in the middle of the pavement and stared up at him, all six feet of rangy blondness. 'I see,' she said softly. 'You're still angling for an invitation to move into Ashton Court, aren't you, Phillip?'

He flushed a little and shifted from one foot to the other. 'It makes sense,' he said defensively. 'There's plenty of room, heaven knows, and I could help keep her company and entertain her——'

'Having you around would drive her crazy in a week.'

'I don't see why it should. She's got you there, feeding you and taking care of all your expenses and——'

'I pay rent,' Sara snapped and turned on her heel.

He followed her down the pavement. 'That's a joke. I'll bet you couldn't live in a cheap boarding-house for what you pay Olivia.'

That was true enough. Sara didn't think it was worth trying to explain to Phillip that it had been a battle to get Olivia to take any money at all.

'And you're not even related. I'm her family,' Phillip said. 'Ashton Court will come to me when she's dead. It has to, because I'm the only heir.'

At that moment, Sara would have said nearly anything to burst his balloon. 'Are you certain of that?' she murmured sweetly.

Phillip's hand closed on her arm and jerked her around to face him. 'What the devil does that mean?' he accused. 'Have you convinced her to leave it to you?'

'If you'll take your hand off me, Phillip——' She stared at him until he released her. 'Of course I'm not working on Olivia to leave Ashton Court to me. What on earth could I do with it, anyway—turn it into condominiums? I just meant that Olivia might have some family of her own——'

'Just Pamela. And she's been gone for years.'

'I mean, besides her daughter. Do you know for certain that she doesn't have any cousins, for instance?'

'No,' Phillip said slowly. 'But she's never mentioned any.'

'That doesn't mean there couldn't be some. And you're only a great-nephew on her husband's side—not really blood relation to Olivia at all.'

He thought that over for a bit, and shook his head. 'But it was Otto who made the money,' he pointed out. 'Strictly speaking, he should have left part of it to me when he died——'

'But he left it to his wife instead. Can't you see, Phillip? It's Olivia's house and Olivia's money, and she can do with it whatever she wants. You shouldn't count on getting——'

'Are you certain you're not taking unfair advantage of her, and influencing her against me?'

'You can do that well enough all by yourself,' Sara muttered. 'Phillip, I think the place is a mausoleum, too—it's grand and wonderful and all that, but it would take all the efforts of twelve people to keep it running in style, and nobody can afford that kind of living any more. What on earth would I do with it, on a college professor's salary?'

He didn't answer, but he continued to look at her suspiciously.

'As far as that goes, why do you want it?' Sara asked finally. 'You're not even married, so you certainly don't need an eight-bedroom house. And insurance agents aren't known for having the sort of income that allows for that style of living. I'm not even sure that Olivia still does. She's been cutting back a bit lately.'

'It's only right that I should live there,' Philip repeated stubbornly. 'She shouldn't treat me like a poor relation.'

They had left the campus behind, and just a block ahead, down a pleasantly busy street, lay the wrought-iron and brick wall that surrounded Ashton Court.

'Damn it!' There was a note of hard disillusionment in Phillip's voice. 'It's not fair. I can't even go inside the gate unless I've got an engraved invitation. And yet I'm the only family she's got. When Otto was alive, I was at least accepted there, and included in the parties. He told me the place would come to me. Olivia's obsessed, you know. She refuses to believe that Pamela's dead, and that's why she just won't admit that I'm the only possible heir.'

Sara looked up at him thoughtfully, and then ahead at the closed wrought-iron gates. Obsessed—it was an unusual word to be applied to Olivia. Fluffy, charming, tiny Olivia—obsessed?

'Pamela was her only child,' she said absently. 'I'm sure it was very hard for Olivia to accept that she's really gone. But surely you don't think she believes that Pamela might turn up some day?'

'Well, they never found a body,' Phillip said bluntly. 'But it's been close to forty years. Any sensible woman would have admitted the facts long ago, but Olivia hasn't. She still pays the premiums on Pamela's life insurance policies, year after year——'

And where insurance was concerned, Phillip would know, Sara thought. She had never realised that, herself. It did seem a little strange for Olivia to do that. Was it possible that, after two years of living at Ashton Court, Sara didn't know Olivia as well as she had thought?

And what about Phillip? She looked up at him through narrowed eyes. If Olivia's late husband had told him he was the heir, had treated him as such, and then instead left everything to Olivia, who wanted nothing to do with the young man . . .

For the first time, Sara felt a twinge of sympathy for Phillip Reynolds. Only a twinge, she reminded herself. But she could understand why he was so upset.

'Just being invited to dinner once in a while would help,' Phillip grumbled. 'You've got no idea what a laughing-stock it makes me in this town, to be Olivia Reynolds' nephew and have less contact with her than the hairdressers on Main Street do.'

Sara pulled open the small wrought-iron gate next to the big driveway ones. 'All right, Phillip, I'll tell her about our talk. But it's up to Olivia, you know.'

'That's the problem,' Phillip called after her. 'Everything is up to Olivia—and Olivia's out of touch with reality!' He turned away from the wall and strode off toward the campus without looking back.

Sara watched him out of sight, and then she walked slowly up the driveway towards Ashton Court. The grounds were so large that it was hard for a guest to realise how big the house really was; the wall enclosed more than half of a city block. A border of pink and blue flowers—a carefully calculated mixture of plants that ended up looking as if they had accidentally grown together—stretched invitingly along the drive. Beyond it, the rosy pink brick of the sprawling house seemed to glow in the summer sun, and the light rippled over the multitude of tiny panes in the casement windows, which stood open to the gentle breeze.

The front door was also open, a dark blur beneath the gothic arch of the entrance. Sara paused for a moment in the dimness of the oak-beamed hall. She might as well tell Olivia right now about her talk with Phillip.

She found the woman curled up on the velvet fainting couch in the small pink and silver morning-room, a crystal cocktail-glass on a table nearby and a box of chocolates balanced beside her. She was engrossed in a book, and Sara stood in the doorway for a long moment, looking at the tiny, white-haired old lady in the frilly, china-blue dress.

Was Olivia obsessed by the loss of her only daughter? Sara wondered. Sara had never suspected such a thing; Olivia seldom mentioned her dead husband or daughter, and she didn't talk about the past. She enjoyed every moment of living, and there was never a hint of the clouds of grief that Phillip seemed to think were hanging over Ashton Court. And yet, that business about her still paying for insurance on the life of Pamela Reynolds, forty years after the girl—woman, Sara corrected herself—was gone . . .

'Hello,' Sara said, at the same instant that Olivia reached for a chocolate. Olivia's hand jerked, and the box went over the side of the fainting couch.

'Goodness, how you startled me, dear.' She sounded faintly reproachful.

'You're jumpy because you read all this junk,' Sara said. She rescued the box of chocolates and picked up the book. The cover was a surrealistic wonder featuring a shadowy figure drenched in gore, staggering down what she supposed was an alley. In big letters was the name of the author—Adam C. Merrill—and on the back was his photograph.

I was right, Sara thought. In person, he's much better-looking than that. Too much so, perhaps, to be credible as an author of this kind of stuff. I wonder if his publisher deliberately chose a picture that makes him look tough.

She turned the book over and looked at the cover again. *Four Fingers From Death*. Where, she wondered, did the man come up with these titles? The last one had been called *Die A Bachelor* . . .

She sighed and put the book down. It worried her sometimes that Olivia read this kind of nonsense. 'It's a wonder you sleep at all, Olivia, with Adam Merrill's murders running through your head.'

'Well, we can't all comprehend Chaucer and James Joyce,' Olivia said, without resentment. 'They're only stories, and they entertain me.' She tucked the book behind a needlepoint pillow. 'There, you don't have to look at it. How was school today?'

As if I was five, and coming home from kindergarten, Sara thought wryly. 'I ran into Phillip this afternoon.'

'Oh? And how is dear Phillip?' Olivia asked brightly.

Sara poked through the box of chocolates till she found a raspberry centre. 'How long has it been since you've seen "dear Phillip", Olivia?' she countered.

'Weeks, I should think.' Obviously it didn't disturb her.

'Well, that's what's bothering him.' Sara summed up what Phillip had said to her, leaving out a few of his choicer phrases; telling Olivia that Phillip thought she was out of touch with reality was probably not going to gain him any points.

'Oh, goodness,' Olivia said. 'I really don't——' She looked at Sara helplessly. 'But if you want him to come, Sara, dear, then of course I'll invite him to dinner now and then.'

'I didn't say I wanted——' Sara stopped abruptly. What does it matter? she thought. I don't think she should keep him locked out of Ashton Court, and if it makes it easier for her to think that I'm in favour of inviting him, what harm can that do?

'On Thursday, perhaps,' Olivia mused. 'Annabelle can do her chicken tourangelle, and I'll invite—oh, we'll have a few people. Twelve or so——'

'I don't think that's precisely what Phillip had in mind,' Sara said drily.

Olivia gave her a brilliant smile. 'Well, if he expects to have you all to himself, perhaps he should ask you out, instead. Surely he can't expect Annabelle to go to all that work for just him? Now that we've got that settled, don't you think you'd best be freshening up? I don't like to shoo you off, dear, but I do so want to finish Mr Merrill's book before dinner.'

'So you have time to let the ghastliest parts of it slip your mind before bedtime?'

'Of course not. So I can talk about it intelligently this evening.' She pulled the book from behind the cushion. 'It's one of his earlier ones—it's just been released in paperback. I can't think how I missed it when it first came out.' She opened the book and looked up. 'Besides, you shouldn't say nasty things about his work, Sara, unless you've read it. Which I happen to know you haven't.'

'And won't. Wait a minute,' Sara said. 'What's going on this evening? It isn't the night for your bridge club, and I can't think of anything on my calendar——'

'We're going to the Talbots' for dessert and coffee, to meet Mr Merrill. Cynthia apologised for the short notice, of course, but she wasn't expecting him till tomorrow——'

'I know.'

'So she's invited a few friends to greet him infor-

mally. I said I knew you'd be delighted, and as for
me, I wouldn't dream of missing the opportunity to
meet one of my favourite authors——'

'Right,' Sara said drily.

'So I simply must finish this before we go. You
understand, don't you, dear? Why don't you wear
that lovely wild-rose dress of yours? It makes you
look so pretty. Oh, and perhaps you will take your
hair down out of the ponytail before dinner?'

It was very gentle. Olivia always was, but her
delicate hints could sometimes feel like sandpaper,
Sara thought. And yet, she really did love Olivia
Reynolds, and as for living at Ashton Court . . .

Was it really just two years ago that Olivia had
invited her to move into the house? Sometimes it
seemed to Sara as if she had always lived here. She
almost said something of the sort, but Olivia had
already put her nose back into her book.

Sara ran up the wide walnut staircase. The evening
sun pouring through the enormous stained-glass
window on the landing smeared jewelled colours
over the pale carpet runner, the carved banister, and
the housekeeper, complete with black uniform, who
was dusting the carved panelling.

'Hello, Annabelle,' Sara told her cheerfully. 'I
might as well warn you; it's chicken tourangelle and
Phillip for dinner on Thursday.'

The housekeeper sniffed. Annabelle had never
troubled to keep her opinion of Phillip Reynolds to
herself. Sara laughed and went on up to her room.

Olivia had insisted that she have the master suite.
'You're giving up so much already by coming to live
with an old lady,' she had said on that long-ago
afternoon when Sara had agreed to move to Ashton
Court. 'You'll need your privacy, and a place to work

sometimes—and a lady's desk should not be in her bedroom.' So Sara had moved into the master suite. She slept in the carved canopy bed of Jacobean oak, and lounged on a love-seat that had graced a French château, and occasionally watched the television set that was artfully concealed in the huge sixteenth-century wardrobe. And, when she brought her students' papers home to read, she marked them in the adjoining sitting-room, on a desk that had once been owned by an emperor.

Not that Olivia had made a serious sacrifice in giving up the master suite; her bedroom next door was quite as elaborate, its bathroom even more sinfully luxurious, and its furnishings, she had once told Sara, all Marie Antoinette. Sara wasn't quite sure whether Olivia had meant the period or the person herself; with Olivia, one never quite knew.

'Personally,' she said to the quiet sitting-room, 'I believe Phillip's a fool. In my opinion, the lady isn't out of touch with anything—she may sound dizzy, but she's as sharp as the average laser scalpel, and I wouldn't care to try to outsmart her.'

She went to shower off the dust of her office. What she would really like to do tonight was put on a comfortable old terry robe and curl up with a good book. She had a new collection of prize-winning poetry that she'd been dying to sample. But years of experience in the academic community had taught her that a mere assistant head of the English department did not insult the president of the college by refusing an invitation to dessert to greet his newest shining star.

Though precisely why Dave Talbot had picked up Adam Merrill and talked him into coming to Chandler this summer was beyond her. Of course, it was a feather in the college's cap to have a best-selling author on campus for a few weeks, but normally Dave didn't dictate things like that. A month ago, however, Dave had come back from his *alma mater's* graduation ceremonies bubbling with enthusiasm about the commencement speaker, and how wonderful it was of Adam Merrill to spend a summer sharing his talents with Chandler's students . . .

His talents, and his ego as well, Sara was willing to bet, after just the few minutes Adam Merrill had been in her office. He probably thought he was a natural teacher—most amateurs did, she had found. And he no doubt expected his students to gather at his feet and listen open-mouthed to his pearls of wisdom . . .

Well, she could cope with anything for five weeks if she had to—even if Adam Merrill turned out to be the worst.

She brushed her hair till it shone like dark honey, and put on the wild-rose dress. Olivia was right; it was the prettiest thing she owned. The delicate shade of pink and the slim lines of the dress with its plunging back showed off the glorious colour of her summer-darkened skin. Not even the guest of honour could turn up his nose at her in that dress, she thought.

Not that she was doing it for his sake, she told herself. Adam Merrill would be a mere shooting star at Chandler College. After the five-week summer session, he'd be gone, and the regular faculty could get back to their ordinary work. And not a bit too soon, she told herself.

CHAPTER TWO

SARA slid a wedge of chocolate cheesecake from the crystal cake-stand on to a glass plate, and looked around the small dining-room where the dessert buffet was set up. Everyone had been served, and from the adjoining living-room came a murmur of contented conversation.

Cynthia Talbot set the silver coffee-pot down and said, 'Get yourself a plate, Sara, and go have a bit of fun. You've been helping me since the moment you arrived, and as much as I appreciate it, you are a guest.'

'But you can't do everything yourself, Cynthia —not with this crowd.' Besides, Sara told herself, it was better to be here, dishing up desserts, than in the living-room, watching half the population fawn over Adam Merrill. Listening to Olivia's barely repressed excitement on the drive from Ashton Court to the Talbots' home had been enough. It had been the final straw when Olivia had caught her first glimpse of him across the Talbots' living-room and murmured, 'I may be an old lady, Sara, but I still know a handsome man when I see one——'

Sara only hoped that he wouldn't be patronising to Olivia, or write her off as a dizzy old lady, not worth his time. That would hurt Olivia beyond bearing . . .

The president's wife laughed. 'I always manage to invite six more people than the house can hold, don't I? I'm too used to the house we had at Dave's last college—it was a drafty old barn of a place, but I could seat eighteen for dinner.' For a moment, she sounded almost wistful.

Sara shook her head. 'That wasn't what I meant. You're a phenomenon, Cynthia. It never seems to bother you, no matter how many people, or how complicated the party——'

'Is that why you're hanging around?' Cynthia teased. 'Trying to steal all my secrets?'

'Well, I have to admit I'd like to know how you're planning to manage a house-guest for the whole summer, yes. Won't you be tripping over him all the time? I thought perhaps he'd rent an apartment or something.'

'Why should he? After all, that's part of the reason the college provides us with a house—such as it is—so we can entertain guests. Besides, every landlord in this town wants a year's lease, and with the housing shortage, they get it.'

That was true, Sara reflected; Chandler's new administration had brought the student population up in a hurry, faster than new apartments could be built. The dormitories were always packed, and every property owner in town had a waiting list. 'I suppose so,' Sara said doubtfully. 'But five solid weeks of a house-guest——'

Cynthia shrugged. 'Dave and I survived three teenagers. We'll enjoy a few weeks with a well-mannered young man around!' She handed Sara a plate. 'Try the walnut torte—it's wonderful, even if I do say it myself. What do you think of Adam? I know you must be excited at the idea of teaching with him.'

Sara opened her mouth, and then shut it again. Just what could she say to the president's wife that would be both safe and true?

'What a perfect opportunity to eavesdrop,' an amused voice said behind them. 'But unfortunately for me, I've been taught that it's impolite to listen in on private conversations.'

Sara spun around. Adam Merrill had come quietly into the small dining-room, cup and saucer in hand.

'Also unwise,' Sara snapped, before she could help herself.

He smiled at her, and his eyes seemed to light from within. But he merely said, 'May I beg more coffee, Cynthia?'

Mrs Talbot refilled his cup. 'I think Sara would enjoy the patio, Adam. There's a beautiful cool breeze tonight, and you've had no chance to get acquainted.'

It sounded like a heavy-handed hint, Sara thought. But Cynthia Talbot wasn't a matchmaker, and Sara fervently hoped that Adam was smart enough to realised that.

'The patio,' he mused. 'The breeze might be refreshing. Shall we sit out there and talk about our class, Sara?'

Yes, she thought, he's smart. He's very smart indeed. Without so much as a direct word to Cynthia, he had made it absolutely plain that it was going to be business, and business only, that occupied them.

Well, she thought, I suppose we'll have to talk about it some time. She meekly picked up her plate and led the way.

The Talbots' house sat high on the limestone bluff that overlooked the river, and the dimly lit patio provided the best vantage-point in town. But apparently no one else had found the view inviting tonight, and Sara was surprised when Adam led her to the furthest and dimmest corner instead of stopping where lights from the house fell into pools across the bricks. He pulled a chair around for her and perched on the patio wall himself, swinging a foot gently back and forth as he drank his coffee. Moonlight glimmered down on the dark water far below them, and cast a blue-black gleam on Adam's hair.

'I appreciate all your help with getting my class set up,' he said finally.

Sara looked up at him over a forkful of walnut torte. His tone wasn't nearly as appreciative as his words had sounded, and her voice was wary as she said, 'My pleasure.'

'But now that I'm here, I'd like to get one thing clear. I'm in charge, and I'll teach the class my way.'

Sara finished her torte and set the empty plate on to a nearby table. 'I don't think you properly heard Professor Mitchell today,' she said mildly.

'But I'm quite sure I heard President Talbot correctly,' he murmured.

'Oh, very good! You think you've trumped my ace, don't you? Well, let me assure you, Mr Merrill——'

'It was ''Adam'' earlier today,' he reminded.

'—that if I could get out of your way, I would. But I'm in charge——'

'I was asked to come here to teach, not to pass out papers for someone else.'

'Have you asked Dave Talbot about it?'

'No. I was hoping we could come to an agreement without dragging him into it.'

Sara stared at him for a long moment, and then said, with a conciliatory note in her voice, 'The fact is, Mr Merrill, I'm responsible for that class, so I'm afraid you'll just have to put up with me. I certainly don't plan to spend all my time leaning over your shoulder and listening to every word. As long as you submit your tests and lesson plans to me in advance, so we can talk about what you're trying to accomplish——'

He shifted impatiently. 'Oh, is that all you want?' he

asked ironically. 'Just approval of everything I do?'

'Look, neither of us likes the idea, but that's the way it is. If I turn my back on that class and you do something crazy, it will be me who ends up in front of the board of regents with my position on the line. Surely you understand?'

'Yes, I think I see now. You're afraid I might be out to get your job.'

'That's not——' she began, in indignation.

'Well, have no fear. I've got no longing to be a full-time teacher.'

'You know, that's one of the things that puzzles me most,' Sara said. 'Why are you here, anyway?'

'I'm fascinated by the challenge of teaching,' he said smoothly, 'and I feel an obligation to pass on some of the knowledge I have so painfully gained through long personal experimentation.'

She thought about that. 'I don't believe a word of it.'

'You don't have a very good opinion of me, do you?'

'I haven't any opinion at all, one way or the other.'

'But why?' he asked softly, as if he hadn't heard her. 'We only met this afternoon. Did you take an instantaneous dislike to something about me? The way I wear my hair, perhaps, or——'

'Of course not,' she snapped.

His eyes glowed again. 'Well, I'm glad that I'm not physically repulsive to you,' he murmured.

'That's not what I said, either,' Sara pointed out.

'Because you're certainly not physically repulsive to me,' he murmured. The violet-blue eyes caressed her face in the moonlight. 'In fact, I could think of a lot of things I'd rather be doing right now instead of arguing with you——'

'Do you fondly believe that I would actually be flattered by that?' She found herself shivering with anger at the very suggestion. 'If you think I'm some inexperienced girl who would be thrilled to capture your attention, you're wrong!'

He shook his head. 'Nothing of the kind. Actually, you made me feel a bit uncomfortable this afternoon; I'm glad you changed clothes. You looked about sixteen, in your jeans with your hair up in that absurd ponytail. You weren't nearly as formidable then, of course, but I've never been a cradle-robber. I prefer a woman who knows what she likes . . .'

'I certainly know what I *don't* like.'

'You're repressed, too, I see,' he murmured. 'What a pity.'

'I am nothing of the sort! Not that it's any of your business. You've got the world's largest ego, Mr Merrill——'

'Don't you think yours is in competition? Within two minutes of meeting me, you decided that I was a hopeless case—certainly as a teacher, and quite possibly as a person as well——'

'And I haven't seen much to make me change my mind since,' she said flatly.

'It's an occupational hazard with teachers, I understand.'

'What is?' Sara scrambled to find the connection.

'Closed-mindedness. In women, I believe, it often shows up as frigidity——'

She was determined not to give him the satisfaction of answering that one. 'You still haven't told me why you're really here. And why Chandler College, instead of one of the big universities?'

'You honestly don't believe that I want to repay my debt to society by passing on my special knowledge?'

'Not for a minute. Is the profit going out of your books, and you have to find another way to make a living? Being on the best-seller list is overrated, I hear—it doesn't always translate into money.'

The violet-blue eyes focused on her. 'I'm awfully glad I didn't give in to the temptation to eavesdrop,' he said thoughtfully. 'It's much more fun to listen to you rip my character apart in person.'

Sara shrugged. 'I'm only asking why someone who was truly successful in your chosen field would agree to spend a summer doing this instead. I think it's quite reasonable to wonder if writing trash is really as profitable as you'd like to have people think it is.'

He laughed. 'Actually, I'm here strictly a favour to Dave Talbot,' he said. 'I'm sure you know how hard it is to say no to that man. If I hadn't agreed, he would have haunted me all Commencement weekend, and I wouldn't have had a bit of fun.'

She nodded, and wondered why it sounded so much like a warning.

'I got fenced into it, but now that I'm here I'm going to give it my best, or else I'm not going to do it at all. So if you don't want to explain to him why I've suddenly packed up and left town, you won't argue with me any more about who's in charge.'

Now there was no doubt about the threat. Well, it didn't bother her—she was only doing her job, and Dave Talbot wasn't an idiot. Sara leaned back in her chair. 'You've made yourself quite clear, Mr Merrill. I'll talk to Dave myself, and save you the trouble. Perhaps he can find someone else on the faculty who would be delighted to give you the liberal atmosphere you seem to need. Hal Mitchell thinks you're wonderful; I'm sure you could work with him——'

She heard a glass door slide open, and with a breath of relief realised that they were no longer alone on the patio.

'By the way, is it just my work you object to, or do you believe that anything which is commercially successful is trash?' he asked smoothly.

'You are twisting my words, Mr Merrill.'

'How do you fit Dickens into that philosophy? Or Shakespeare? They both wrote for the money, and nobody's calling their work trash.'

'Here they are, Olivia,' Dave Talbot's deep voice boomed. 'We thought you two had gotten lost somewhere—probably on purpose.'

'We were discussing our differing philosophies of the flaws in modern literature,' Sara said, with a look at Adam that challenged him to deny it.

He smiled and said nothing.

'Literature,' Dave Talbot snorted. 'What's the matter with you, Adam? A dark patio, a full moon, and a lovely woman, and you're talking about literature?'

'Mr Merrill was giving me the benefit of his first-hand experience with the subject,' Sara murmured.

A flicker of irritation in Adam's eyes told her that the barb had not gone unnoticed, but he was too busy arranging a chair for Olivia to retort.

'Well, give it a rest, Sara,' Dave ordered. 'We don't pay you enough to make you work all the time, you know. Enjoy yourself——'

'I didn't know you were such a chauvinist, Dave. The moon, the dark and a woman, indeed!' she chided.

'That's not chauvinistic, that's common sense,' he defended cheerfully. 'You did seek out the dark, you know. It seemed a natural conclusion to draw.'

'He's got that kind of reputation, has he?' Sara said under her breath.

Olivia leaned forward in her chair. 'Sara, dear, I've asked the Talbots to bring Mr Merrill to dinner at Ashton Court on Thursday—to the dinner party you wanted me to give for Phillip.'

'Don't you think you'd better invite Phillip first?' Sara said, a little tartly. 'He is supposed to be the guest of honour.'

Olivia shrugged. 'Oh, if he's busy then, we'll have him another time.'

Sara bit her tongue hard. Adam had resumed his seat on the patio wall and was watching her with interest. She knew his eyes were on her because of the odd little tremor that kept running up and down her spine, even though to all appearances his attention was focused on Olivia.

'And do come early, so there's a chance to stroll through the gardens,' Olivia told him. 'The flowers are so lovely just now.'

'I'm sure I'll love everything about your home,' he said.

Sara fought off a little shiver at the charm in his voice. He certainly appears to be a gentleman, she thought, and Olivia was eating it up. It should have been a relief to know that he hadn't snubbed the old woman. He could well have written her off at a glance as a harmless nut who could do him no good. And yet, Sara didn't feel quite comfortable about the whole thing . . .

'How did Ashton Court get its name?' Adam asked, as if he really would like to know. Olivia seemed to glow a little. She settled herself with a little flounce in her chair, smoothed her pearl-pink chiffon skirt, and began to tell him about all the years she and Otto had worked and planned and dreamed of the home they would build, once Otto's factory was a success.

Sara could repeat the story by heart, so she turned back to Dave Talbot. He sipped his Manhattan and said, 'Hal Mitchell and I are looking forward to some good things coming out of that class you and Adam have this summer. I talked to a few of the students at registration today. They're really excited about it.'

Sara said, carefully, 'I was thinking, Dave—it really won't take both of us to handle that class. Mr Merrill is well qualified——' She thought she heard a choked-back laugh from the patio wall, and carefully avoided looking at him. 'If I was relieved of the responsibility of that class, I'd have time to help students with some special projects——'

Dave Talbot was shaking his head. 'No, no. I wasn't going to say anything till we saw how this summer works out, but actually, Sara, we're hoping to make this a regular part of our curriculum. Get other writers in here, at least one a year, to give our students the benefit of real-life experience. Hal doesn't have time, so you'll be co-ordinating the whole show. It'll be a wonderful opportunity for you to learn, too, sharing a classroom with people like Adam.'

Just terrific, she wanted to say. Adam Merrill had given up all pretence of listening to Olivia, and was staring at Dave Talbot as if he'd been stabbed in the back.

Well, Sara thought, it was a good thing I've got that class outline ready to go—because it looks as if I'll inherit the whole thing, as soon as he regains his voice and tells Dave he's leaving . . .

Olivia was prattling on. 'And of course, Ashton Court was a wonderful place to raise a family. There was always room for all of Pamela's friends. She brought them home to skate and to swim and to sleep over, when she was little——'

She hasn't even noticed yet that no one's listening, Sara thought.

Adam Merrill was staring at Sara, and his face looked as if he'd been chipped out of a glacier.

It's not my fault, she wanted to scream at him. *I tried!*

She saw him swallow hard and close his eyes for an instant, as if he was in pain, and she waited for him to tell Dave Talbot, in some devastatingly frank language, just what he thought of this new twist. It ought to be worth hearing, she thought, even if it will be quite a shock to Olivia's ladylike ears . . .

And then, instead, he turned to Olivia, and said gently, 'Your home must be a beautiful place, with all the love you've poured into it. I'll look forward to seeing it on Thursday.' He patted Olivia's hand, tenderly. 'And now I think perhaps we'd all better go back in. It's getting late, and I see that Sara's shivering.'

It was such an anticlimax that it kept her awake half the night, thinking about it. Of all the reactions Adam Merrill could have displayed, calm courtesy was the one she would never have expected. She eventually concluded that he had simply controlled his temper because Olivia was there, and waited till the guests were gone before talking to Dave Talbot. It's probably all over by now, she told herself sleepily, watching as the shadows cast by the full moon crept across the Persian carpet in her bedroom.

So she was astonished when Adam came into her office the next afternoon, without bothering to knock, and pulled a chair around next to her desk so he could straddle it and fold his arms on the back.

'You're still here,' she managed to say, and felt incredibly foolish.

'Surely you didn't expect me to act last night without a chance to think things out, did you?'

'And now that you've thought?'

'Oh, I'm staying.'

'Did you manage to convince Dave that my presence

in your classroom would stifle your creative energy?' Her voice was tart.

'No. He convinced me that you could take over a lot of the tiresome paperwork and leave me free to bend my ingenious brain to teaching——'

'I'm here to teach,' she quoted him crisply, 'not to pass out papers for someone else.'

He ignored the interruption. 'And he assured me that you would be most helpful and always willing to pitch in.'

'Dave's a better diplomat than I gave him credit for. What happened to your grandiose threat to leave if you didn't get your way?'

'I decided in the middle of the night that you're a small price to pay for five weeks of free room and board.'

'I imagine the Talbots are thrilled at that news,' Sara said faintly.

He grinned. 'Oh, I didn't put it quite that way to them, of course. But you know how it is for us struggling writers of trash—we have to take advantage of our opportunities.'

'Enjoy your little joke.' She pulled another folder out of the filing cabinet and absently threw most of its contents away without a glance.

'After I've had a chance to think about it,' Adam mused, 'I believe you might just come in handy, now that Dave's made it clear who's boss. It'll leave me a little free time to do my own work—I'm beginning to think this town might make a good setting for my next book. Olivia's place sounds like a wonderful site for a murder. By the way, do you live there, too?'

'Yes. Why?' she asked crisply. 'Do you have me in mind to be the victim?'

'It had crossed my mind. Is she your grandmother

or aunt or something?'

'No. Just my friend.'

He shook his head admiringly. 'Nice work, if you can get it. And you think I've got a nerve to take advantage of the Talbots for a few weeks!'

'I am not taking advantage of——' She stopped suddenly, and decided she didn't have to explain anything to Adam Merrill.

'Do you think she'd mind if I used Ashton Court as a setting?'

'I doubt it—she thinks you're wonderful. But why don't you ask her?'

'I will. There aren't any nice little mysteries hovering around this town, are there?'

'Looking for an inspiration for another masterpiece? *Murder at Ashton Court*, perhaps?'

'What a plebian title. I was thinking of *The Facts of Death*, myself. Has there been a juicy axe-murder, or an exciting triangle where the betrayed husband did away with the lovers, or an embezzling scheme that ended in a faked suicide? That would be good.'

'None of the above,' Sara said. She pushed her horn-rimmed glasses up on her nose and went back to sorting papers.

'I don't require a happy ending, by the way—or any sort of ending at all, actually. Just a starting-point. I have plenty of imagination to take care of the rest.'

'I didn't doubt it for an instant. But I can't think of a single thing you might be interested in.'

'Fine lot of help you are,' he grumbled. 'I suppose there's a courthouse here?'

'Right in the middle of the town square. You can't miss it; it looks like a gothic castle. Why?'

'Old records. You can't have a crime without leaving a paper trail. And usually there's someone around who remembers the scandals and skeletons. I'll start asking people who have lived here for ever. I'll bet Olivia knows——'

Sara looked up in shock. 'No! Don't for heaven's sake ask Olivia!'

'Why not? She'd be ideal. She must have lived here for a hundred and three years——'

'Just don't, that's all.'

He let the silence drag out for a long moment. 'Really, Sara,' he said reasonably, 'you can't give me that kind of an order and not explain it. I'll be certain to put my foot in it the first opportunity I get.'

She sat up straight in her chair and looked at him over the top of her glasses. 'On purpose, I suppose.'

'If I must.' He propped his elbows on the back of his chair. 'Come on, give.'

She sighed and put her glasses down on the desk blotter. 'Look, I really mean it. She's an old woman, and it's painful enough for her without having someone probe forty-year-old wounds. Will you promise, if I tell you everything I know, never to mention it to her?'

He raised a dark eyebrow. 'Would you trust me if I promised?'

'Probably not.'

His smile flashed. 'In that case, I'll promise.'

Sara gave up. 'She mentioned her daughter to you last night.'

He frowned. 'Pauline, or something?'

'Pamela. By all accounts, Pamela was an indulged child who became an impossible young adult—running with the wrong crowds, giving her parents ulcers, doing all the ridiculous things kids did forty years ago and adding a few twists of her own for good measure. There was nothing Otto and Olivia wouldn't do for her, or give her, but by the time she was a teenager, she rejected everything they stood for. If they liked something, Pamela didn't. If they disapproved of a young man, Pamela went out of her way to make friends with him. She was a spoiled-rotten brat who set out to make life miserable for her parents.'

Adam patted back a yawn. 'So what happened? I'm afraid I don't quite see——'

'When Pamela was a freshman at Chandler College, she vanished one weekend. She told her room-mate she was hitch-hiking into Chicago to see a concert because her father had told her she shouldn't go——'

He sounded incredulous. 'If she had everything she wanted, why was she hitch-hiking?'

'Otto had just put his foot down—for the first time ever, I gather—and taken away her car because she was flunking three subjects, and he'd caught her drinking and driving.' Sara picked her glasses up again. 'She was seen several miles east of town, getting into a battered old black car with a young man of unsavoury appearance, and she's never been seen since.'

'Oh.' Adam sat very still, thoughtfully. 'And the young man in the car?'

'They never found him. Do you know how many battered old black cars there could have been in this state? Besides, it was three days before anyone realised she was missing, and the young man probably had nothing to do with it at all.'

'If her father had just disciplined her,' Adam said thoughtfully, 'she might have simply run away.'

'Perhaps. She was of legal age, and that was the first thing the police considered. But she took practically nothing. She even left a wad of cash in her dorm room, along with all her clothes and her personal belongings—

and a partly written research paper that was due the following week.'

'That doesn't sound like an intentional disappearance,' he admitted.

'Not for a student like Pamela, at any rate. She wouldn't have bothered to do her homework at all if she didn't intend to turn it in. There was not the slightest bit of evidence that she didn't plan to come back.'

'And in all these years——' Adam sounded unsatisfied.

'Nothing. Not a word, not a sighting, not a hint of what might have happened to her. The police finally concluded that she must have been murdered, probably for what money she was carrying. There's a lot of rough country between here and Chicago; she could be anywhere.'

'Not a very tidy ending,' he mused.

'No. Otto and Olivia kept private detectives working for years, before they finally gave up——' Sara remembered what Phillip had said yesterday, about Olivia's obsession. Had she ever given up? Or did she still look, and hope, and just not talk about the search?

'Not very satisfying, somehow,' he went on. 'Surely, there is something more out there, waiting to be found . . .'

Sara watched him for a long moment with growing horror in her eyes. He had folded his arms across the back of the chair and rested his chin on them, and he was staring past her and out the window with a distant expression in those strangely coloured eyes, as if he was looking at a Chandler College of forty years ago . . .

'Look,' she said uneasily, 'I only told you all that to keep you from nagging Olivia about it. It's certainly not a fit subject for a book——'

'Why not?' he interrupted.

'Because there isn't any answer to it.'

'Are you certain of that? Who knows what loose ends might be lying around, just waiting for someone to give them a tug?'

'You wouldn't! Adam, please, Olivia told me all this when she invited me to move in with her because she thought it was only fair that I know. I think I'm probably the only person she's ever shared it all with, and if you start digging around in it . . .'

'If I dig, it will be very quietly.'

'I don't think you realise what a small town this is. Everybody knows everything that happens, or at least enough to fuel gossip——'

He waved her concern away.

'Besides, I don't see what you could do after forty years that wasn't done at the time.' She felt as if she was grasping at straws.

'It probably doesn't matter, anyway,' he said.

'Good. I'm glad you're seeing sense——'

'It's only the idea I need, not the details. And I think——yes, I think this could be it.'

But surely, Sara thought, with any luck, he'd be long gone by the time the idea came to anything. And even if he used it—well, didn't it take years sometimes to get a book written and published? Olivia might never see it at all . . .

At least I can hope, she thought. And if I hadn't told him, he would have asked her, and that would be worse.

He looked at her, finally, and smiled. 'I see why Olivia might be a bit touchy on the subject of crime, though. I'll be very careful.'

'And yet she reads your books without turning a hair,' she said thoughtfully. 'I think it's a bit gruesome, myself, to drench yourself in books about the very kind of nightmare that destroyed your life.'

'Gruesome?' he asked with cool politeness. 'Do you actually believe that's a more respectful way to refer to my work than to call it trash? Have you ever read any of my books?'

'No, but——'

'May I suggest that you do, before you say anything else nasty about them?'

She watched him warily for a long moment. Sometimes, she told herself, you're just not very discreet. 'I'm sorry. I got a bit carried away, I think.'

'If you're looking for trash,' he went on, 'I would suggest that you start by sending your precious creative-writing textbook to the dump.' He gave her copy a push with a contemptuous finger.

She bristled at the challenge, and forgot about Pamela. 'It is the most widely used work in the field today.'

'By professors who don't know any better, and students who haven't any choice. How many books has that author written? Not textboks; I mean real live novels that people buy off the supermarket racks?'

'He doesn't write that kind of thing. He's a scholar.'

'And do you know why? Because he's incapable of writing a book that would sell to the popular market. He can't string a sentence together and make it interesting. What the hell good is a textbook that puts its readers to sleep?'

'If you're finished with your lecture, Mr Merrill——'

'I'm not, so if you're going to try to defend the pompous idiot who wrote that abomination, don't bother.'

'I suppose you could do better.'

'I certainly couldn't do worse!'

'And what are you going to call it?' she asked sweetly. *'The Gospel According to Merrill?'*

He grinned, abruptly, and the rancour died out of his eyes. 'Not bad,' he said, and reached out to shake her hand with elaborate politeness. 'You know, Sara Prentiss, in the next five weeks, I may be able to turn you into an opponent worth considering, after all.'

CHAPTER THREE

ADAM went off down the hall to his own office, whistling, and Sara spent the next half-hour head-first in the waste-basket, retrieving all the papers that she had absent-mindedly thrown away while she was talking to him.

My hands were certainly busy, she thought, while my brain was working on something else. What is there about the man that short-circuits common sense in the people around him?

Dave Talbot was a good example, she thought. It was apparent that Adam had worked some sort of conjuring trick on him, and, unfair as it might be, Sara was struck with the consequences.

'And I might as well make up my mind to be a good sport about it,' she told herself firmly.

It was after five when she locked her office. The long halls of the liberal arts building were empty and echoing, but the door of the office Adam was sharing was open, and he was sitting at a table by the window, his dark head bent over a yellow legal pad.

'Getting your opening lecture in shape?' she asked, leaning against the door.

He looked up with a grin. 'No. I've been writing limericks and waiting around for you to catch me looking studious, so you could be impressed with my industry. Now that you've seen me at it, I'm ready to go home.' He tore the top sheet off the pad, folded it and struck it into his shirt pocket, and picked up his linen sports jacket. 'See you tomorrow, Ernie.'

The man at the other desk in the room looked up, said, 'Humph,' and turned back to his book.

'I don't think Ernie likes me,' Adam confided as they walked down the hall.

Sara choked back a smile at his innocent expression. 'For starters,' she said sombrely, 'I've never heard anyone call him "Ernie" before in the three years I've been at Chandler. It's always "Professor Ryan", so it's no wonder if he's not impressed with your casual attitude.'

'I'm not much impressed by him, either. He hums.'

'So? You whistle.'

'Yes, but I whistle on key, and not while someone else in the room is trying to concentrate.'

'I thought you were only writing limericks.'

'Listen, do you think that's easy? It took all my efforts to come up with a rhyme that made sense.' He fumbled in his pocket for the slip of paper. 'It starts out, "There was a professor named Prentiss——" '

'I don't want to hear it.'

'Just as well. It's not finished yet, and if Ernie doesn't stop humming, it probably never will be.'

'I'll speak to Ernie.' She caught herself. 'Professor Ryan, I mean.'

'You have my deepest gratitude.' He held the door for her.

'And I'll tell him to keep humming.' She gave him a saccharine smile.

He looked wounded. 'See you tomorrow in class.'

Sara grumbled under her breath.

'Eight o'clock. Nice of them to give us a bright and early start, wasn't it?'

She didn't bother to answer. At the edge of the car park, she paused and looked up at the sky. The afternoon had grown sultry, with the promise of a

summer rainstorm, and one glance at the clouds told
her she would be prudent to hurry on her walk back to
Ashton Court if she wanted to avoid a drenching.

'I'll give you a ride home,' he offered. 'It's the least I
can do for my assistant, after all.'

'You're planning to enjoy this, aren't you?'

'Every minute of it.' He opened the door of a shiny
white Corvette.

Sara looked thoughtfully at the name painted on the
sign marking the parking spot. 'This is my reserved
space,' she pointed out.

'I know,' he said agreeably. 'That's what gave me the
idea to write the limerick, you see. It's a very unusual
spelling.'

'You aren't supposed to park here.'

'Why not? You weren't using it.'

'That doesn't mean I never want to use it again.
When it's nice weather, I walk sometimes, but——'

'The point is, you don't have a car today, so what
does it matter if I used your space? Are you going to get
in, or shall we both stand here and wait for the clouds
to burst?'

She got in. 'Please don't take my parking place again,
Mr Merrill.'

'I've been meaning to talk to you about that, too. Do
you think you could possible stop calling me Mr
Merrill? It makes me feel about seventy-four years old.'

'I'm so sorry it gets on your nerves,' she said with
exaggerated politeness.

'But you made such a good start yesterday. I thought
we were going to be the best of buddies, and then
suddenly you went all formal on me, and turned my
hopes for a close relationship into dust——' He looked
as if he was about to cry.

Sara glared at him. 'If you're rehearsing for an

Academy award, please don't waste it on me. I am unmoved.'

'All right,' he said cheerfully. 'If you're going to be stubborn, I'll just start calling you Dr Prentiss again. But it makes me want to stick out my tongue and say "Aaah" every time I say it.'

'Different sort of doctor,' she reminded.

'I know. But I'm afraid if you keep this up I may start to get an uncontrollable urge to take my clothes off whenever I'm around you——'

'Enough,' she announced. 'I concede—Adam.'

He was the most unpredictable person she'd ever run into, Sara thought. He was like a stray beam of sunlight bouncing through a mirror-lined room—it was impossible to guess from what direction he'd pop out next. Was this his normal personality, she wondered, or was it just the excitement of the new challenge? He might even be a bit worried about the class, she supposed, and this was the way he reacted to stress. But she hoped this sort of quicksilver behaviour was the exception. If he was like this all the time, she was going to have a headache for the next five weeks . . .

No sense in dwelling on that, she told herself. 'This is a very nice car,' she said instead.

'Yes, it is, isn't it? I had a windfall. People seemed to enjoy throwing money away on paperback trash last years, so I sank it into the car.'

Sara chewed her bottom lip and finally said, 'Look, would you stop reminding me of that? I've told you I'm sorry about calling your work trash.'

'Oh, I don't have any hard feelings about it,' he assured her. 'I accept your professional opinion of my work. You've got a bunch of letters after your name, so of course you know best.'

She glared at him.

'There's only one tiny thing——' he asked, in the hesitant tone of someone asking an enormous favour. 'Would you actually read some of it before you issue any more critiques?'

There was no winning an exchange with him, she reflected. And on that issue, she supposed he had a point. The only sensible thing was to refuse to argue with him. Fortunately, they didn't have far to go. 'Ashton Court is on your right.'

He slowed the car at the corner of the wall, and as he caught a glimpse of the house he whistled. 'Nice little place,' he said. 'Funny, but when Olivia said something about Ashton Court last night, I thought at first she was talking about a mobile home park. I still haven't figured out why she called it that, you know.'

'Long gone ancestors,' Sara said briefly. 'Thanks for bringing me home; I'll get out here.' She had spotted Olivia's bright red gardening hat in the midst of the front flowerbed.

'Are you trying to ditch me? I wouldn't want Olivia to think I'm anything short of gentlemanly, you know, and dropping you off in the street just wouldn't be done by the best people.'

The wrought-iron gates stood open, and before Sara could gather another argument the little car had flashed between them and pulled up at the front door.

'Besides,' Sara said, 'you saw Olivia, too.'

He grinned. 'Of course. Why should I miss a chance to improve the acquaintance?' He sprang out of the car as if he was going to rush around to open Sara's door. Instead, he ignored her and headed straight for Olivia.

The old lady looked up from her bed of pink delphinium and held out a hand to check for raindrops. 'How nice of you to bring Sara home, Adam,' she said. 'Can you stay and visit with us? Run along inside, both of you, and have a drink, and I'll be in as soon as I've finished tying these plants up.'

'I couldn't think of leaving you to work out here in the rain,' Adam said. 'If you'll show me how to help——'

Sara groaned and climbed out of the car. 'So much for gentlemanly conduct,' she muttered, and went to pitch in.

They were all slightly damp by the time the flowers were finished, but Olivia was glowing with pleasure. 'I certainly didn't plan to turn you into a gardener,' she told Adam with a smile. 'But you've got a natural touch with delicate things.'

'So I've been told,' he said soberly, but Sara thought she could see a gleam of mischief in his eyes.

What kind of delicate things? she wondered. Nothing that was suitable for describing in mixed company, she'd bet. She didn't realise that she'd indulged herself in a kind of snort until Adam directed a reproachful violet-blue gaze at her.

'I'll get some ice,' she said quickly, and retreated to the kitchen.

When she came back, Olivia was giving him the first-class tour of Ashton Court's formal rooms. Sara poured herself a glass of sherry and curled up in a wing-backed chair in the little pink and silver morning-room. Olivia's guided tours sometimes took hours, and Sara wasn't foolish enough to follow along behind on this one. So she sat quietly and stared at the portrait of Otto that hung above the fireplace. He had been a handsome man, distinguished, white-haired, upright, with none of Olivia's soft fluffiness. There was firmness in his jaw, and determination in his eyes. And, though he was smiling, there was sadness in every line of his face, as if he never knew true happiness any more.

I don't suppose he did, Sara thought, after Pamela was gone.

The thought of Pamela brought her straight up in her chair. Adam had said he would be careful, she remembered, not that he wouldn't talk to Olivia about that old story. Why had she ever trusted him alone with the old lady?

Footsteps crossed the hall, accompanied by a trill of laughter, and Sara relaxed. You're just too darned suspicious, she thought.

'Sara, dear?' Olivia said. 'Oh, here you are. You must get so tired of listening to me go on and on about Ashton Court. Of course, I realise it isn't the thrill to anyone else that it is to me—I can't walk through a room without remembering the hours we spent in planning it, and the two years it took to build it.'

'It's a beautiful house,' Adam said.

Olivia's smile was tremulous. 'They tell me I shouldn't stay here, that it's too big for me, but . . . May I get you a drink?'

Adam's eyes focused on the glass in Sara's hand, and she would have sworn that he had to stifle a shudder. 'Whatever you're having is fine, Olivia,' he said firmly. He propped an elbow on the back of Sara's chair and said, under his breath, 'And tell me, Sara, dear, just what did you have to do to be invited to live here?'

She frowned at him, and he subsided into silence and studied the portrait above the fireplace with an abstracted air.

Olivia crossed the room with two martini glasses. There was a flicker of surprise in Adam's eyes as he took one.

Sara smiled. 'You expected to have to drink sherry?' she asked softly.

'Otto and I never did succeed in acquiring a taste for

sherry,' Olivia said mildly. 'Sara likes the stuff, so of course if you'd rather have that, Adam——'

'No, this is fine.' He tasted the drink. 'You certainly developed a talent for mixing martinis, Olivia.'

'Much more my style, I'm afraid,' Olivia said, as if she was a bit ashamed of herself. 'Sara's tried to improve my tastes, but I'm afraid it's too late for that.'

'I've been wondering how you two got together,' Adam said. He propped an elbow on the marble mantel.

'He means, because we're such an unusual pair,' Sara murmured to Olivia. 'And I warn you, Adam's curiosity is unbearable—not only for him, but for whomever he's curious about.'

Olivia laughed. 'Actually, you're wondering how I got such a treasure, aren't you?' she asked Adam. 'Simple enough, really. When Sara first came to Chandler, she wasn't very happy——'

And Olivia can't take a hint to save her soul, Sara thought. She interrupted smoothly. 'Olivia helped me through a tough time that first year while I got used to a small town and a small campus.'

Olivia blinked at the unusual rudeness, and then nodded. 'That's right,' she said. 'Before she came here, Sara was——'

'Used to a much more active life,' Sara went on. 'We became friends, and of course when Olivia felt she needed someone to be in the house with her at night, I was happy to help out.'

Adam smiled. 'I'll just bet you were,' he said admiringly.

'Now she's as dear to me as if she was my own niece.' Olivia smiled.

'How charming. Do you have a collection of aunts, Sara?'

She sent him a cool smile. 'Sorry to disappoint you, Adam. No aunts.'

'And since she doesn't have any family of her own left any more, it's worked out wonderfully for both of us,' Olivia said.

'I can see that,' Adam murmured.

The smooth innuendo irritated Sara. How would he know about the pain of being an only child, orphaned before her tenth birthday? And how dared he belittle her feelings for Olivia? The old lady's friendship, so freely and generously given, had helped to fill the horrible, aching space left when the grandmother who had raised her, the only anchor left in Sara's world, had died when she was in college. Let it pass, Sara, she told herself. He wouldn't understand, anyway.

'Tell us about yourself, Adam,' she suggested. 'The jacket of your books does an excellent job of preserving your privacy.'

'You got that far in reading one of them, did you?' He took a sip from his martini. 'I'm amazed.'

'Yes,' Olivia said eagerly. 'Please tell us, Adam. I've always wondered about you. You're such a young man to have achieved so much success.'

'I had an early start.'

'Where are you from, Adam? Who are your people?'

'My father is a Protestant clergyman in Virginia.'

Sara was unaware that she had made any sound at all, until he looked at her with raised eyebrows. 'It's an enlightened branch of the church,' he said.

She glanced at the martini he was holding and thought about his books. 'It must be,' she said. 'Or else I'll bet you don't go home very often!'

'And your mother?' Olivia asked. 'She must be a very special woman to have raised a son like you.'

'She is—she's a surgical nurse at a hospital there.'

'Oh, that accounts for your fascination with blood and weapons——' Sara began.

Olivia gave her a quelling glance, and said, 'What do you think of Chandler, Adam? We're very proud of our college, here.'

'You should be.'

'Which means,' Sara said gently, 'that he's astonished to find anything so progressive in such a small town.'

'I didn't say that.'

'But you were thinking it. Didn't Dave Talbot tell you it was started as an experiment by a prominent educator? It's always been slightly ahead of its time.'

'There really was a Mr Chandler?'

'Oh, yes. Mr Chandler was an old friend of the educator's. He donated the money for the whole quadrangle, but never set foot in the state, much less on campus. They did that a lot in those days.' She shrugged. 'At least he had good taste in architects. What about your education, Adam?'

'You sound like the ladies who used to come to the manse for tea, you know,' he said. ' "And how are you doing in school this year, Adam?" ' he mimicked.

'Sara,' Olivia said warningly. 'I'm sure we don't want Adam to feel that we're prying into his private life.'

'No, but I'd certainly like to know if his education was entirely self-acquired,' Sara said unrepentantly. 'If I'm going to be in a classroom with him——'

'How do you think I got invited to give a commencement speech at Dave Talbot's university? Because I graduated from there myself, that's how.'

'After studying what?'

'Political science.'

'Well, I knew it couldn't be literature. That's an

awfully broad field, Adam; what did you intend to do?'
She raised her eyes to his over the rim of her glass, and
suggested gently, 'If you don't want to tell me, there
are other ways I could find out, you know.'

He said, sounding reluctant, 'My major emphasis
was the politics of ecology, actually.'

Sara choked on her sherry. 'The politics of *what*?'

'It's a perfectly valid field, you know. The disposal of
solid waste ought to be a concern to every thinking
citizen. It's just that it's impossible to make any money
doing the long-range planning for how we're going to
dispose of all the garbage this country will generate in
the next fifty years, and so——'

She couldn't help it. She looked up at him, absolutely
straight-faced, and murmured, 'So you took up another
form of trash instead.'

'Sara,' Olivia chided, 'that's not very kind of you.'

Adam grinned. 'That makes two I owe you.' He
saluted her with his martini glass, and set it down on
the glass cocktail-table. 'And perhaps I should warn
you, Sara, my dear, that I always pay my bills.'

Adam was already in the classroom when she arrived
the next morning at two minutes to eight. He was
sitting on the edge of the desk, swinging his feet and
talking to the half-dozen students that had already
gathered. On his knee was a hardcover copy of
Everlasting Murder, open to the title page, and he was
gesturing with a fountain pen.

It's a fan club, Sara thought irritably the moment she
walked in. And, at this hour of the morning, I'm not
equipped to deal with it . . .

He looked up with a smile. 'I was wondering if you
had decided to sit the day out entirely.'

'Of course not.' She popped the plastic lid off her

polystyrene container of coffee and took a sip, grimacing at the taste of the muddy fluid. Not even cream and sugar could disguise the inky taste. Why couldn't the faculty lounge produce real coffee? she wondered. She had overslept, and there hadn't been time to make a pot at Ashton Court.

'Oh, I know what it is, now,' Adam said cheerfully. 'Hal Mitchell told me that you hated early classes. But don't you know, Sara, my dear, how happy the rest of us are to see you? You're beautiful when you're half-awake. Most women, on the other hand——'

There were a couple of stifled giggles from the students. Sara ignored them and said sweetly, 'I'm sure you have a lot of experience.'

Adam grinned. 'Quite a lot, yes.' Then he added innocently, 'My mother worked nights for years, and she still doesn't attempt to communicate in the mornings. And my two kid sisters——' He shook his head. 'It's horrible the sight they are at dawn.'

'This isn't exactly dawn. But I'll admit to not being at my best till afternoon.' She looked for a place to set the cup down. Adam was occupying a great deal of the top of the small desk; he was apparently absorbed in autographing the book at the moment, and didn't seem to notice that she needed a bit of space. Finally, Sara gave up and took a student desk at the corner of the room. I can supervise just as well from here, she told herself firmly.

He watched thoughtfully as she distributed the careful outline of assignments and tests, and then said to the students, 'You're here to increase your ability to write, and the only way to learn is to do it. Everyone in this room has a certain amount of talent, even Dr Prentiss——'

'Gee, thanks,' Sara muttered.

'The key is whether you've got the stamina to stay with it, and the drive to keep writing even when it seems nobody wants to read your stuff. Five weeks isn't very much time for this kind of class, so we're going to spend it in writing, not studying for exams and reading textbooks——'

A student in the front row said, looking baffled, 'Then what's this for?' He held up the outline.

'To make Dr Prentiss feel useful,' Adam said kindly. 'You'll probably get something of the sort from her now and then; feel free to ignore it. Oh, since you've each got a copy of that thing, let's put it to good use. Turn it over and use the blank side to tell me a little about yourself and why you're taking this class.'

Sara sat silently and fumed while he spent the next hour discussing his approach to writing. The monumental ego of the man, she stormed inside, while she sat quietly and with every appearance of polite attention. He then suggested that before the next day's class they write about a personal experience that had changed their lives, and finished up by saying, 'We aren't going to have enough time to accomplish everything we want to do. Shall we agree to start class a half-hour earlier every day, so we can all get the maximum benefit?'

Sara was stunned when the class agreed. She was still sitting in her corner when the students had all filed out and Adam finally slid off the desk. 'I've never seen anything like it,' she muttered. 'A group of kids agreeing of their own free will to get up a half-hour early to come to class . . .'

Adam shrugged. 'I don't suppose you'll admit that it's my scintillating personality that makes them want to hover around?'

She shook her head. 'That's impossible. It must be

that you promised them no tests.'

He reached for her coffee-cup. 'What have you got in here?' he asked, studying the dregs. 'It's made you positively disagreeable. Shall we go find you an antidote?'

'I can't. I've got a rhetoric class to teach at ten.'

'What a shame.' He dropped into step beside her.

'That I can't listen to more of your lecture?'

'I'll come to yours instead,' he offered. 'I'll be happy to help out a little here and there.'

'No, thanks.'

'Then I'll see you tomorrow. Do you mind if I use your office for a while?'

Sara stopped. 'You have an office of your own,' she reminded.

He smiled at her as if she was a particularly wise child. 'Yes,' he agreed. 'But Ernie's probably there. Besides, yours will give me the proper atmosphere to work on my limerick.'

What Olivia insisted on calling 'Phillip's dinner' had turned into an extravaganza, as parties at Ashton Court had a habit of doing. There were going to be fourteen for dinner, Olivia had announced breezily at breakfast on Thursday morning. Sara, who was still half asleep, poured herself another cup of coffee and said, 'Are you certain you couldn't think of anyone else?'

Olivia frowned. 'Is there someone I've forgotten? But it's too late to invite anyone else, I'm afraid. It's only a small party, anyway.'

'Small? Compared to what?'

'Oh, we used to have house parties for that many,' Olivia said. 'For weeks. Sometimes when Otto's customers visited the plant, they'd bring their families along to stay at Ashton Court. And I used to have

garden parties for all our friends. Every year, at the end
of summer, until . . .' For a moment, she looked almost
haunted, and Sara held her breath. Then Olivia seemed
to shake herself back into the present. 'Dave Talbot is
going to act as host tonight, by the way. It's such a
nuisance not to have a man at the head of the table.'
She sounded almost fretful about it.

'Don't worry about it. With or without a host, all your
parties are wonderful, Olivia.' Sara sipped her coffee
and pushed the cup aside. She'd have to dash or she
would be late, and Adam had better not have taken her
parking spot this morning, or he'd really have
something to answer to, she thought. 'See you this
afternoon.'

Olivia leaned across the table, the filmy sleeve of her
pale pink négligé dragging against the blue linen cloth,
and put a small box next to Sara's plate. It was wrapped
in silver paper and topped with a pale blue bow.

'What's this?' Sara said warily. She had an idea, of
course; at least once a month Olivia did something of
the sort.

'Just a little trinket I found yesterday.'

Olivia's last 'little trinket' had been an antique lead
crystal vase for Sara's room, big enough to hold a dozen
long-stemmed roses with ease; she blithely ignored the
fact, Sara thought, that roses by the dozen were not
sent to Sara's door with any regularity . . .

'Olivia,' she said unhappily, 'you know I wish you'd
quit doing this.'

'But why should I stop something that gives me so
much pleasure? Go ahead, open it.' She settled back
into her armchair with satisfaction to watch.

The little velvet-covered box sprang open to reveal a
gorgeous white-gold dinner ring. In the centre was a
step-cut sky-blue stone, surrounded with diamonds.

Sara stared at it for a long moment and then looked up at Olivia. 'You know I can't possibly take this,' she began.

'But why can't you, darling? It's only aquamarine, and the diamonds are just tiny ones,' Olivia said practically. 'And I know how you love jewellery.'

'Well, I haven't time to argue about it now, that's sure.'

Olivia reached for the box. 'Good. I'll have Annabelle leave it on your dressing-table so you can wear it tonight. Tell Adam how much I'm looking forward to seeing him, would you, dear?'

Sara tried again that evening to make Olivia see sense. As soon as she was dressed, she knocked on the woman's door, and went in with the box in her hand.

Olivia turned from her dressing-table, where she was expertly applying make-up. I hope I look so good at eight-two, Sara thought, half enviously. Olivia's was a fragile beauty, but a very real one.

'Sara, you look lovely! I thought when you bought that dress that ivory would be a good colour for you, but I had no idea——'

'Olivia, darling, I came to talk to you about this.' Sara set the velvet box on the glass-covered table.

Olivia's lower lip trembled. 'You don't like it, then?'

'I love it, but——'

'Then please accept it. You do so much for me, my dear, and I like to see you have pretty things while you're young and can enjoy them.'

Meaning, Sara thought, that when she was my age she had nothing much at all, and certainly not jewellery. And the daughter she would have liked to give these things to is forever gone . . .

'It would please me so much,' Olivia murmured. Her soft hand patted Sara's. 'Wear it for me tonight?'

And just how could she refuse that request? 'All right,' she said. 'I'll wear it tonight. But I'm not accepting it as a gift.'

'Why not? It's just the colour of your eyes. You keep it a while and think about it, dear.' Olivia turned back to her mirror.

Sara sighed. That whole exchange got me precisely nowhere, she thought. The woman is impossible; she simply will not listen to reason!

She tried to slide the aquamarine on to her right ring finger, but it balked at her knuckle. She tried the other hand, and the ring slid firmly into place.

Phillip was already in the drawing-room, standing by the front windows with his hands clasped behind him, rocking back and forth on his heels and staring at the Impressionist painting of a riverbank that hung above the fireplace.

He looked over his shoulder at her and said, 'Have you any idea what kind of money Olivia's got tied up in furniture around this place?'

Sara closed her eyes for an instant and said, 'Hello, Phillip. It's a pleasant evening, isn't it?'

'I suppose that means you don't want to talk about it.' He turned back to stare at the painting. 'Why do they consider him an artist, I'd like to know? I'd think any kindergartener with a set of watercolours could make the same bunch of dots on paper?'

'Perhaps you should get married,' Sara recommended drily. 'If you had enough kids producing pictures, you might even be able to afford to live at Ashton Court.'

'You're laughing at me,' he said. 'Well, not everyone has the same taste in art.'

And very fortunate that is, too, she thought. 'Would you like a drink, Phillip?' She moved across to the cart and poured herself a glass of sherry.

'Bourbon and soda, please. You know, Sara, what you said the other day about turning this place into condos—I think it could be done. I'd forgotten how enormous it is.' He ran an experienced eye over the dentil moulding at the top of the room.

Sara shivered a little. 'I'd advise you not to say anything of the sort in front of Olivia.'

'Why not? I'd be careful to tell her that it was your idea, not mine. It might just be a little encouragement to be sure Ashton ends up in the right hands.' He took the glass, sipped, and looked at her thoughtfully. 'Though, as far as that goes, perhaps you had a better idea a minute ago. If we were to agree to get married, Sara, we could solve this whole squabble about what happens to Ashton Court. What do you think?'

CHAPTER FOUR

SARA took too big a gulp, and for a moment she felt as if she'd swallowed the glass instead of the sherry. 'Is that actually a proposal?' she asked faintly, and sat down in a wing-backed chair, feeling the need of a little support.

'I said "if",' Phillip reminded.

'Oh.' She began to see the humour in it. 'I'm glad you made yourself plain.'

He leaned on the back of the chair and bent over to watch her face. 'Well? What do you think of the idea?'

'I'm afraid I was raised by a grandmother straight out of the Victorian era,' she said, keeping her composure with difficulty. 'She always told me never to consider the possibility of a proposal until it was actually made, so——'

Phillip looked confused.

The doorbell chimed discreetly, and a moment later Annabelle came into the drawing-room. 'Mr Merrill,' she announced in her nasal twang. She cast a sour look at Phillip and vanished back toward the kitchen.

'Sorry to interrupt,' Adam said breezily. 'But I thought it was going to be a party tonight. If I'd known it was only a twosome——'

Sara jumped up, glad of the excuse to escape Phillip's smothering presence. 'Olivia will be down in a minute. I don't mix a martini as well as she does, but I'm willing to try. Have you two met? Adam Merrill, Phillip Reynolds.'

Phillip looked down his long nose and said, 'Welcome to Ashton Court, Mr Merrill.'

60

Sara swallowed a groan. Really, she thought, Phillip makes it sound as if his name is already on the deed!

Olivia came in with a soft swish of powder-blue taffeta. 'Adam,' she said, holding out her hands to him, 'it's so nice to have you here!'

He smiled down at her and raised both of her hands to his lips. 'It is my privilege, Olivia.'

She gave a little crow of delight. 'And I'm glad to see you, too, Phillip,' she said.

Sara thought Phillip looked as if he was having a stroke.

'You're alone, Adam?' Olivia questioned. 'I thought surely Dave and Cynthia would be the first to arrive——'

'They got a telephone call from their daughter just as we were ready to leave the house,' Adam said. 'So they suggested I come along with their apologies. They'll be here any moment.'

'I knew it must be important; they are such thoughtful people. Though of course if Dave didn't show up at all, I'm sure I could shanghai someone else into acting as host.' Olivia patted Adam's sleeve and smiled up at him.

Phillip cleared his throat. 'I'd be happy to do my duty, Aunt Olivia.'

Olivia looked at him with distaste. 'I certainly wouldn't want you to think of it as a chore, Phillip, dear,' she began.

Sara said, quickly, 'Didn't you say you wanted to show Adam the garden before it gets dark, Olivia?'

'Yes, I did——'

As if on cue, Annabelle came in again, this time with a stoop-shouldered old gentleman with a walking-stick, one of Olivia's long-time friends.

Olivia looked disappointed for an instant, and then

she said brightly, 'Sara, dear, why don't you take both Adam and Phillip out to see the gardens? It's been so long since Phillip was here that he would enjoy it too, I know.'

'Are you just visiting in town, then?' Adam asked pleasantly as he set his half-full glass aside.

'No, I just haven't happened to be at Ashton Court for a while,' Phillip snapped. 'What of it?'

Well, Sara thought philosophically, if they come to blows in the garden, at least there won't be bloodstains on the Aubusson carpet in the drawing-room . . . She drained her sherry-glass and fleetingly wished she could sneak another. 'Gentlemen?'

It was something like a royal progression, she thought as they crossed the lawn to the formal rose garden. She stumbled once on the flagstone path; her high-heeled shoes weren't intended for outdoor exploration. Adam caught her arm and then drew her hand into the crook of his elbow. Phillip, not to be outdone, took her other hand.

'Nice ring,' Phillip said. 'I didn't notice that the other day.'

'It's a dinner ring,' Sara said. 'I don't wear it for ordinary occasions.' And if you expect me to tell you where and when I got it, she added to herself, you're a bigger fool than I thought, Phillip Reynolds.

'Well, I suppose you can afford that kind of thing, since it doesn't cost you anything to live,' Phillip said.

Adam's eyebrows went up.

'I don't know why Olivia insists on keeping you here,' Phillip went on grumpily.

And to think that just minutes ago he was thinking of proposing, Sara chided herself. Sara Prentiss, you've got no luck whatsoever when it comes to men!

'Perhaps,' she said sweetly, 'she thinks it's wise to

have a chaperon around.'

Phillip frowned at her. 'What on earth do you mean?'

'Don't underestimate Olivia,' she advised. 'I wonder sometimes if she's thinking of marrying again.'

'Why would you suspect such an idiotic thing? The woman is ancient!'

'But not dead,' Sara pointed out. 'Didn't you get the feeling, when she suggested we leave, that she was sending the children out to play so the adults could talk in peace? She and Simon have been friends for years, you know.'

They walked on in silence for a few yards, past the small imitation of a Greek temple that sheltered the swimming pool. She pointed the grass tennis court out to Adam. 'It hasn't been kept up for a while, though,' she said regretfully. 'It's easier to play at the country club, and I'm beginning to think that Olivia is feeling the financial strain of keeping Ashton Court up. She never talks about it, but one of the gardeners quit this spring and she hasn't replaced him . . .'

'I believe I'll go back inside,' Phillip said. 'The mosquitoes are starting to bite.' He dropped her arm and hurried away.

They strolled on toward the roses. 'Have you seen any mosquitoes?' Sara asked, after a moment.

'No,' Adam said soberly. 'But then, neither of us would be as delectable as Phillip is. His skin is really regrettably thin.'

She started to giggle.

'He looked a bit green, too, don't you think?' Adam went on remorselessly. 'Perhaps he's allergic to the little devils.'

She doubled up laughing and dropped on to a stone bench at the edge of the garden.

'And speaking of little devils, Sara Prentiss, you are

one. I'm shocked at your remarkable performance!'

'I couldn't resist it,' she managed to say. 'And he reacted so well——'

'Possessive sort, isn't he?' He sat down beside her and picked up her hand. 'At first I thought it was you he was scrapping over.' He held up her hand and admired the aquamarine. 'When I came in tonight, Phillip was bent over your chair as if he was about to kiss you, and he looked quite unhappy at being interrupted. I thought perhaps he'd just put the ring on your finger.'

'No. Sorry to disappoint you, but——'

'But now I see that it would be totally out of character for him.' He turned the ring back and forth to watch it catch the light. 'If Phillip were to propose, he'd probably give you a desk pen or an unabridged dictionary or something equally practical.'

'It's funny that you should say that,' Sara said demurely. 'As a matter of fact, he'd just mentioned marriage when you came barging into the drawing-room. I'm to think it over, and consider all the advantages of sharing Ashton Court with him.'

He patted her hand and put it back in her lap. 'I'd think long and carefully,' he said judiciously. 'And I'd be cautious about putting all my eggs in one basket.'

'Don't worry. Phillip's not my choice of basket.'

Adam's eyebrows arched. 'Why would I be worried?'

'Why, you——' she snapped. 'As if I was implying that I—that you——'

He interrupted smoothly just as she sputtered to a halt. 'Would you like me to tell you how I spent my afternoon?'

'I can't imagine why I would want to know,' Sara said in her nastiest tone, 'but I'm sure you're going to tell me, anyway.'

'I've been cultivating acquaintances at the local banks.'

'Oh? I suppose you need a loan, despite the free room and board?'

He reached out and plucked a cream-coloured rose from the bush, stripped the thorns off it, and tucked it into the clasp that fastened her hair behind her ear. 'Did you know,' he said casually, 'that Pamela Reynolds still has a current account at First National Bank and Trust?'

For an instant, Sara thought her head was vibrating, and then she realised that Annabelle had struck the dinner gong on the terrace. She jumped up.

Adam looked startled. 'Is Olivia that much of a stickler on promptness?'

'No, but Annabelle is. She's been with Olivia for ever, and we couldn't possibly do without her if she ever got mad enough to retire. Tell me about the bank account. Does Pamela actually use it?' she asked as they retraced their steps to the house.

'It's been inactive for years,' he admitted.

Sara thought it over for a long moment. 'Then I can't see that you've discovered so very much.'

'How can you say that? In one day's time I've discovered a whole lot more than you have in two years.'

But they reached the house just then, and Adam was caught up in introductions, and there was no more time to discuss it.

Nevertheless, it was the only thing Sara could think of all through dinner. She scarcely tasted the chicken tourangelle, and as she ate her strawberries with cream she found her gaze resting on Adam more often than was comfortable, wondering how he had managed to get that information, and what else he might have found out. Weren't bank accounts a confidential matter? But, of course, if it was a female whose acquaintance he was cultivating, he might have persuaded her to overlook that minor detail, she thought drily.

'She's not really seriously ill, you see,' Cynthia Talbot said to her, across the table. 'It's only minor surgery, but it's a concern, nevertheless. Dave needs me here, and yet she is my daughter, after all, and I feel that I should help out.'

'Of course you must do what you think is right,' Sara said absently. 'And you know we'll all pitch in and do whatever we can to help.'

Cynthia looked at her for a long moment, and then smiled. 'Sara, you've got such a way of putting things in perspective,' she said.

Is that what I did? Sara wondered idly. And to think I did it accidentally, at that.

Olivia ran an old-fashioned house, and when the ladies retreated to the drawing-room for their coffee, the gentleman stayed in the dining-room. Sara had a bad case of fidgets by the time the men appeared, and she caught Adam's eye the moment he came into the room and tilted her head meaningfully toward the terrace. He responded only with one slightly lifted eyebrow, but five minutes later he joined her there. The wait had felt more like a year to Sara.

'Finally,' she said in relief when he closed the french doors quietly behind him. 'I thought you were never going to show up.'

Adam grinned. 'I'm terribly flattered that you want to be alone with me,' he murmured. 'Shall I kiss you now, or may I drink my coffee first?'

Sara's jaw dropped. 'I don't——That wasn't what I had in mind at all!'

'I'm sorry I didn't get the hint earlier, Sara, my dear.'

'Will you get it through your head that I'm not hinting?'

His eyes were warmly appreciative as his gaze skimmed over her body. And even though he hadn't touched her—had never touched her in any more intimate way than to take her arm as they walked in the garden—she found herself tingling from head to foot, as if every square inch of her skin was being caressed by a lover's hand.

That's impossible, she thought. I stopped feeling those things years ago. And I don't plan to ever get caught in that trap again.

'Are you certain?' He sounded doubtful. 'You got rid of Phil very efficiently before dinner.'

'It's not the same thing at all,' Sara snapped. 'I don't have any particular interest in you. I want to know more about Pamela's bank account.'

Adam sipped his coffee. 'What a pity,' he said. 'Dave Talbot's right, you know. A patio, a moon, and a lovely woman, who only wants to talk about a bunch of old money—what a waste!'

She turned her back on him. 'All right, don't tell me.' She folded her arms defiantly.

He chuckled, and she heard the click of china as he set the cup and saucer down. 'If I share my information,' he warned, 'I'll expect you to share yours.'

'I don't know anything more than I've already told you,' she protested softly.

'You may have picked up important things that you don't even recognise, just by being around Olivia.'

'I don't think so. But all right—anything I know, I'll share.'

'I'll hold you to that,' he said softly.

'Now will you answer my question? Is there a lot of money in that account?'

'No. A couple of hundred dollars.'

'And it hasn't been touched in years?'

'It has been thirty-four years since the last cheque was written, to be precise.'

Sara frowned. 'But surely——'

'I know. You're wondering why the bank hasn't considered it an abandoned account by now, and closed it out.'

'That occurred to me. Besides, they have a monthly service charge at that bank—it would have eaten up the balance long ago.'

'Yes, if there hadn't been regular deposits into it.'

'Deposits?' She stared at him.

'Always the same amount, at regular intervals—just enough to make up for the service charges.'

'But why? Do you mean that Olivia's been keeping it open deliberately?'

'It was the only possibility that occurred to me.'

She sighed. It was beginning to sound more and more as if Phillip was right, and Olivia was obsessed by the possibility that Pamela was still out there somewhere. 'I can see why she would do it,' she said slowly. 'Originally, I mean. If Pamela did run away, sooner or later she'd need cash, and she might try to get that money—it belonged to her, after all. It makes sense that Olivia would have left that account alone, and kept an eye on it——'

'For thirty-four years?'

Sara sighed. 'That's the other thing that bothers me. Phillip told me that Pamela's been gone for forty years.'

'That's quite a discrepancy,' Adam admitted quietly. 'Could Phillip have been simply exaggerating? He seems the type to make more of something than it really is, and he can't be old enough to remember the whole fuss.'

'No.' She thought about it and added, 'I mean, he's in his early thirties, so he wasn't even born till afterwards. But——'

Adam sighed. 'I'll work on it. I suppose the local newspaper has microfilm records of their old issues? With the possibility of having to go through six years of newsprint, I should be done in—say, eight months or so, if I haven't gone blind first.'

'I could ask Phillip,' Sara offered half-heartedly.

'That's a good girl—you pump Phillip for a little more information, and then I'll know where to start looking.'

'But he'll ask why I need to know.'

'I have confidence that you can figure out a story.' He looked down at her and added thoughtfully, 'You know, you aren't half bad at writing fiction yourself. That tale about Olivia and her friend with the walking-stick——'

'Simon?' Sara laughed. 'That's not fiction. He comes regularly. They drink old-fashioneds and play cribbage and talk about people I never knew.'

'People like Pamela?'

'I don't know,' she admitted softly. 'Usually I retreat to my sitting-room and grade papers. Adam, do you think this is such a wonderful idea? It's prying into Olivia's private life, just for the sake of curiosity. I really think you'd better not go any further.'

'I thought we were partners.'

'I've changed my mind about it.'

'That's not playing fair. I told you about the bank accounts.'

'And I told you the whole story in the first place. Adam, if Phillip is right, and Olivia actually does believe that Pamela's still alive, it could even be dangerous to interfere.'

'Dangerous?' he scoffed. 'How?'

'It might unbalance her—how should I know? But I think we should drop it right here.'

He shook his head. 'I disagree.'

'What are you trying to do, anyway?' Sara asked in exasperation. 'Solve the mystery and win Olivia's undying gratitude? She already thinks you're a saint——'

'That's not a bad idea,' Adam mused. 'Maybe if I succeed, I could move in here, too.' He looked up at Ashton Court, where moonlight glimmered against soft-coloured brick and slate tiles and leaded windows. 'You did make a promise, you know.'

She fought a battle with her conscience. She had promised, that was true, and he'd kept his part of the bargain. 'All right, I'll ask Phillip when it happened. But that's all.'

'That wasn't what I meant, actually. You said you'd answer my questions if I'd answer yours.'

'And I told you I didn't know anything else!'

'Oh, I think you can answer this one. Where did you get the ring, Sara? And why is it on that finger?'

She looked up at him in honest amazement. 'What's that got to do with anything?' she asked.

'I didn't actually say that every question I wanted to ask you concerned Pamela,' he reminded. His face was half-shadowed, half-moonlit, and his voice had a tinge of huskiness in it.

Almost unwillingly, she whispered, 'Olivia gave it to me. And it wouldn't fit on my other hand——'

There was silence for the space of a breath, and then Adam said, 'Then it's all right for me to do this.' His hand cupped her face, and drew her, very gently, close to him. The first touch of his lips on hers was almost like a butterfly's kiss, soft and light and tender. Sara's eyes fluttered closed and her mouth softened and opened under his. His arms went round her and his kiss became a demand, not harsh or vicious, but with a sort of confidence in it, as if he tasted willingness within her, and expected that inevitably, whatever he asked, she would give . . .

The moment I met him, Sara thought hazily, I wanted this to happen . . .

The thought sent a sort of aching panic straight to Sara's heart. I can't, she thought. I can't let it happen again!

She pulled away, her hands to her face, trying to rub away the impact of his kiss. 'It's not all right!' she gasped. 'How dare you think that I wanted——'

'Because you did,' he said. He was breathing a little faster than normal himself. 'And for a minute, everything was all right—better than all right. You kiss like an angel, has anyone ever told you that? What the hell happened, anyway? It was like biting into a marshmallow and finding a seed in the middle——'

'You think I'm a marshmallow, is that it?'

'That's not quite what I said——'

'Some sort of pushover, then? I suppose you thought I'd rush right off to bed with you.'

'I didn't invite you to do that, no.' He leaned against the back of a stone bench, his arms folded, and a spark of humour flared in his eyes. 'Where do you think we could go, anyway? I doubt Olivia's that enlightened, and I suspect that the Talbots aren't, either. Besides, the walls of their house are like cardboard, and frankly, I'd prefer a little more privacy while I get to know you.'

'You aren't going to do any such thing,' Sara snapped.

'Are you certain you mean that? For a moment, I thought I was the one who was being seduced, Sara.'

Hot colour was washing over her face, and she

turned away, biting her lip. A fool, that's what I am, she told herself helplessly. All he wanted to do was give you a harmless kiss, and now you've turned it into a world-class disaster.

No, she thought. It was more than just a harmless kiss, far more. He was trying to keep you off balance, so you wouldn't interfere with his little mystery problem.

She huddled into herself, her arms crossed. The summer breeze suddenly felt chilly, and the thin fabric of her dress was not adequate protection against the cool air, or the weight of Adam's gaze. She shivered.

'I'm sorry I teased you,' he said, and his voice was suddenly deeper, and very serious. 'You're obviously very unhappy about something, and I've just made it worse. Will you tell me what's wrong?'

She shook her head. She wouldn't look at him; she just wanted him to go away.

'You've been here at Chandler for three years,' he said thoughtfully. 'And you've got your doctorate—that means you must be twenty-seven, maybe twenty-eight years old.'

'You flatter me,' she said. Her voice shook a little.

'You aren't going to convince me that you've reached that advanced age——' there was a tinge of laughter in his voice '—without ever having been kissed. And even if you tried to tell me that, I've got first-hand evidence that it isn't true—you certainly know how to do it properly. So it isn't inexperience that terrified you.'

She shuddered a little.

'And I refuse to believe that I frightened you. I took particular care not to. I hope you appreciated my consideration.'

'Would you just let it rest, Adam?' Her voice was taut.

'No, I'm afraid I can't.' It wasn't unkind, just matter-of-fact. 'So that leads me to conclude that you've had a rotten experience somewhere along the line.' He paused thoughtfully. 'I wondered why you were so careful not to let Olivia tell me about you yesterday. Pure rudeness it was, and that's not like you. At least, not towards Olivia.'

'Don't you ever forget anything?' she said bitterly.

'Rarely. So you're here because of a man——'

She clenched her fist and held it tight against her mouth. Every muscle in her body was tense.

'Want to tell me about him?' he offered genially.

'No, I don't.' Too late, she realised what she had admitted. 'Adam, would you just so away and leave me alone?'

There was a long, thoughtful moment. 'I'll go away,' he said finally. 'If you insist. But I don't plan to leave you alone. You're full of riddles, Sara Prentiss. And the one thing I never could resist was a good puzzle.'

She didn't turn around for a full minute after she heard the tiny creak of the french door closing behind him. Then, with a shudder that racked her body, she sat down on the stone bench, folded her arms on the back of it, and buried her face.

He'll take me apart, she thought, and turn each piece upside-down until he knows every detail. He's relentless, and he already knows too much. How did he see all that? Am I so very obvious?

In three years, she thought hopelessly, no one else has so much as asked. Even Olivia accepted what I told her, and didn't ask for more. No one else has suspected that there was any reason for me to come here except that Chandler College offered me a good job. Where else could I be the assistant head of the English department, and a full professor, at twenty-nine? That's reason enough for me to be here.

But it was not enough to satisfy Adam Merrill, she thought hopelessly. He would probe until he found out what he wanted to know, because his own ego would make it impossible for him to believe that the truth might be much simpler—it might be that she simply didn't find him attractive.

But she did, she had to admit. That was where the problem had started; he was too darned attractive, and for an instant, when he had kissed her, she had forgotten that she had made up her mind never to trust a man—any man—again. Logical, independent, self-sufficient Sara Prentiss didn't need a man. And no man would ever take advantage of her again, the way that Guy had . . .

Just thinking of Guy brought her to her feet, pain gripping deep into her body. Guy had used her and played on her vulnerability. He had been the shining light of the academic community at the university she had attended, the author of what would some day be the world's greatest novel, the wounded soul that only Sara could understand and appreciate—at least that was what he had told her. And then, in the end, he had betrayed her.

It was your own fault, she told herself. You were a silly, gullible fool then. But it will never happen again. Never again will you listen to a glib tongue and believe . . .

Certainly she would not allow herself to be vulnerable to someone like Adam Merrill, who had demonstrated his glibness without any doubt. Just getting himself invited to spend the summer at Chandler, and to stay with the Talbots, was evidence enough, to say nothing of the way he'd ingratiated himself almost instantly with Olivia, as soon as he'd found out that she had money and position in this small community . . .

Five weeks, she thought, and he'll he gone. Perhaps he was only bluffing when he said he wanted to figure out the puzzle about me, because I offended him, and bruised his ego. He's got plenty of other things to do. The class will take up most of his time . . .

She paused. She couldn't entirely avoid going to class, that was sure.

'I'll just stay away from him,' she muttered. 'I'll go to class, because I must, but I'll stay quiet and I won't get into arguments with him. I'll just avoid being alone with him, and before I know it, the weeks will fly by and he'll be off somewhere else, and I can settle back into real life.'

Starting, she told herself, by getting back inside to the party, before everyone began to wonder what had become of her. She smoothed a hand over her head, half surprised that, despite the explosive quality of that kiss, not a single strand of her hair was mussed. That's Adam's experience showing, she thought. He may not have invited me to go to bed with him, but only because I didn't give him a chance.

She slipped quietly through the french doors and across the little den to the drawing-room. No one seemed to notice her as she slipped through the crowd; that was a bit of relief, she thought. No one, she amended, except Adam. His eyes flicked over her without expression and then returned to Olivia, but Sara thought she could detect a little softening in his face, a tiny relaxation of his shoulders, as if he was relieved.

He was probably half afraid I was going to use my belt to hang myself from the oak tree behind the house, she thought irritably. As if I'd do anything so foolish because of a man . . .

Once, she had considered doing that, she remembered, when Guy's betrayal was fresh, and she didn't think she could face another day without him. And then she had realised that what she really dreaded was facing the people who had known the truth. They had known that he was making a fool of her, but they hadn't warned her. So she had held her head high despite her pain, and then she had come to Chandler and buried the past . . .

'Of course,' Olivia said. 'It's the only thing that makes sense. Don't you agree, Sara?'

Obviously, Sara thought, I've missed out on an important part of this conversation. 'I'm sorry, Olivia—I didn't quite catch what you were saying.'

'I've solved the problem. Cynthia's going to go get her grandchildren and bring them home with her—someone's got to take care of them, the poor dears, while their mother is ill. But that means she'll have her house full. So Adam's coming to stay here at Ashton Court for a while.'

Sara's eyes, wide with shock, met Adam's across the room. She expected to see triumph in his violet-blue gaze, but it wasn't there. She wondered what was going through his mind, and found herself thinking, he didn't even have to solve the mystery to get his invitation . . .

CHAPTER FIVE

THE PARTY broke up soon after that, and Sara went to her room in an exhausted daze. But sleep didn't come, and eventually she threw the sheets back and went to sit on the window-seat with her feet drawn up under her, looking out over the rose garden and idly drawing patterns on the glass with a fingertip, watching the aquamarine in her ring sparkle in the moonlight.

It was funny, she thought idly, how it could all come back in a flash—memories that she had thought were long buried and past. She had got over Guy years ago, but how quickly it had all come back tonight, fuelled by a simple kiss . . .

It was odd, she realised, that it had been Adam's kiss which had raised the spectre of Guy, when Phillip's half-proposal earlier in the evening hadn't. For Adam's direct, methodical habit of going after what he wanted was most unlike Guy, while Phillip's way of suggesting everything, while committing himself to nothing, was just the sort of thing Guy Bradford had been an expert at, she reflected. He could have written a book on indirectness . . .

Sara had been doing research for her dissertation when she had met Guy in the university library one Sunday afternoon. She knew who he was, of course, this brilliant professor and author of a stunning first novel that had set the literary world on its ear. The whole campus knew that he was working on a second, a blockbuster book, but no one knew what it was about.

It was at Sara Prentiss's table that he chose to work that quiet Sunday afternoon. And when, an hour later, his papers intruded on her space, he gathered them up with a boyish smile, and apologised, and introduced himself—quite shyly, as if everyone on campus didn't know who he was. She was charmed by his modesty . . .

And that was how it had all started. Such a simple beginning, she thought, staring out at the silvery flood of moonlight over Olivia's roses. And I was such an innocent fool, and lonely, because I'd just lost my grandmother. A perfect target.

It had quickly become a habit for them to spend Sunday afternoons sharing a quiet table at the library. Sara didn't quite know when she had stopped thinking about symbolism in sixteenth-century verse and started thinking about Guy Bradford's big brown eyes, but it had been early. And when one day he'd invited her to have coffee with him and talk about their work, she hadn't hesitated for a moment . . .

She knew he was married, of course. But her friendship with Guy had nothing to do with that, she told herself. Theirs was an intellectual, stimulating relationship—the kind he could never share with his wife, he had confided sadly. His wife simply wasn't able to understand his work, to comprehend the pressure that a writer lived under—not as Sara understood . . .

'You were a gullible fool,' she told herself.

They had started spending Sunday afternoons at her apartment, where the university gossips—who also wouldn't understand the purity of their friendship —couldn't see. Soon he was spending much of his time there, even when she was in class, because it was quiet and he could work on his book. When she came home, they drank coffee and talked. And ultimately, one night, he had stayed . . .

As soon as the book was finished, he told her, they could get the rest of the mess straightened out. He would tell his wife, then—not that it would be a surprise, he said, because they hadn't had much of a marriage for years. But he couldn't take a chance on his university position until the book was finished. The book would be their security, their ticket to a new life. Then they wouldn't need to worry about what anyone else thought, but in the meantime they would have to keep their love a secret.

Sara had believed. For nearly a year she had thrown herself into making his life smoother, so he could work on the book. Then one day she had gone unexpectedly to a university function and had seen Guy there, with his adoring wife—a woman who was not only very pretty, but who was undeniably and gloriously pregnant, as well.

She had gone straight back to her apartment, and for the first time in a year she had opened the drawer in her desk where Guy stored the novel-in-progress. She had spent the rest of the afternoon reading the most disorganised mass of tripe she had ever encountered. What he had been doing with all his time, she didn't know, but he certainly hadn't been writing a book. By the time Guy arrived with flowers, her illusions lay in tatters. There wasn't a blockbuster novel in his future, and for her there wasn't much future left at all. She had shredded the flowers and packed his things herself so that he'd had no excuse to linger, and a few months later, when the job offer had come from Chandler College, she had seized it, and not looked back . . .

Until now, she thought. Odd that tonight it had all come back to her, because of a simple kiss in the moon-

light. Or perhaps it wasn't so odd; perhaps the little
voice of reason in the back of her mind was screaming a
warning. What did she know about Adam Merrill, after
all, except what he had told her? She had taken Guy
Bradford on faith, and he had betrayed her. It had taken
years to get over him, and she would never let it
happen again.

Thank heaven for Olivia, she thought. Without ever
asking a probing question, Olivia had known that Sara
had been deeply wounded. The old lady who could
appear so dizzily disconnected had been the one who
quietly pushed Sara into the social life of Chandler
College and the town, inviting her to Ashton Court to
lunch, to dinner, to parties. It was Olivia, Sara was
convinced, who had engineered her appointment as
assistant head of the English department last year;
Olivia had no position of authority at the college, but
she wielded a great deal of strength in her gentle way.

Now Olivia had invited Adam Merrill to Ashton
Court as well. And there was nothing for Sara to do but
put up with it. She could endure Adam Merrill, but the
one thing she couldn't bear was to hurt Olivia.

She was purposely on time to the minute the next
morning, to avoid any need to talk to Adam before
class. She wheeled her tiny car into the car park and
screeched to a halt near her parking place; there was a
shiny white Corvette in her spot. By the time she found
a place on the street and walked half-way across
campus to the liberal arts building, she was distinctly
late, and class had already started.

Adam pointed that out to her when she came in.

'You should be glad I wasn't carrying a switchblade
this morning,' she retorted. 'I'd have gleefully slashed
your tyres!'

After class, he dropped into step beside her. 'Are you avoiding me?'

'I can't think why you'd have got that idea.'

'I don't want to bother you, but——'

'Good.'

'May I use your office today?'

'Why not use your own?'

'Ernie. Every now and then, he breaks out in some foreign language. Is he having a religious experience, or what?'

'It's only Middle English. He's teaching Chaucer this semester, and he had to get himself back in voice to read it in class.'

'Oh. I was half expecting men in white coats to come and sweep him up any minute.' He snapped his fingers. 'It's not Ernie who's the man in your past, is it?'

'Professor Ryan? Don't be absurd.'

'Well, he didn't seem your type,' Adam said reasonably. 'On the other hand, I can't imagine——'

'Any man who is my type?' Sara interrupted drily.

'That wasn't what I meant. But he doesn't seem to like you any better than he does me, so I thought perhaps he was carrying a grudge.'

'He is. He's been here for decades, and he thinks he should have my job. I was promoted over his head.'

'A youngster like you, taking away the man's dream,' Adam chided. 'You should be ashamed. So tell me about the man in your past.'

'No, thanks.' She paused at the door of her classroom and turned to face him. 'If you'll promise not to take my parking spot any more, I'll let you use my office.' She dangled the key over his outstretched hand.

'Do you expect me to park my precious toy on the street?'

'Why not? You drive it there.'

'Tell you what, he offered, 'after this, I'll give you a ride every day. That way we'll both be on time.' He pushed a lock of honey-coloured hair back behind her ear and traced the line of her jaw with a careless finger.

A student ducked around them and into the room, with a surprised look. Sara groaned. 'Would you stop it, Merrill? You're going to have my students thinking we're dating!'

'Do you want me to straighten them out?' he asked. 'I'll be happy to come in and tell them we're not dating at all. As of this afternoon, we'll be living together.'

He moved into Ashton Court on Friday afternoon. Sara had purposely avoided her office and gone downtown instead to take care of some errands, and by the time she got home the entire atmosphere of the house had changed. She knew he was there the moment she walked into Ashton Court; she could feel his presence in the air, even though Adam was nowhere to be seen.

She found Olivia arranging flowers in the butler's pantry.

'Your embroidery thread, madam,' she said dramatically, and handed over a tiny paper bag.

Olivia set a bunch of daisies down unceremoniously and opened the bag. 'Thank you, dear. I had my doubts that you'd be able to match it.'

'So did the proprietor of the shop, but we managed to find some in a corner where it must have been hiding for years. Where's your house-guest?' she asked, keeping her voice carefully casual. 'I expected him to be in the kitchen by now, charming Annabelle by eating cookies at a furious rate.'

'He's unpacking. I've given him the guest-room at the head of the stairs. It's the most comfortable one,

and there's a desk there—I'm sure he'll want a place to
set up his typewriter. Isn't he a charming young man,
Sara?'

Yes, Sara admitted to herself, he is, but that's not
quite the only adjective I'd choose to describe him.

'He said now he understands how an unwanted child
must feel—being shifted around like this.'

Sara thought, as if he could possibly know how it
feels!

'Can you imagine Adam being unwelcome anywhere, Sara? I told him that of course we want him——'

Speak for yourself, Sara wanted to say. 'Olivia, I'm
sure he was only teasing you.'

'Perhaps, but I'm very anxious that he feel
comfortable. I've told him to make himself right at
home here at Ashton Court.'

'I'm sure he'll do that,' Sara muttered.

'It will be so nice to have a man around the house,'
Olivia said cheerfully. She cut an inch of stem off a
daisy and placed it just right in the cooper bowl.

She's talking about it as if it's a permanent arrangement, Sara thought. I wonder if Adam is hoping to
make himself indispensable around here so that when
the summer is over, Olivia will ask him to stay on.

Don't be silly, she told herself tartly. You're just
touchy because of that kiss last night, and because,
instead of apologising this morning like any decent man
would, he made it even worse. Carrying on like that in
the halls of the liberal arts building, for heaven's
sake—this has got to be stopped. You'll just have to tell
him that his conduct isn't particularly wise, that's all.

The door of his room stood ajar. She tapped on it,
and it opened under her hand.

Adam grinned at her. 'Olivia said she wanted me to
feel welcome, but I didn't expect this!'

'I just came up to make sure you had plenty of towels and everything,' Sara said, determined to keep her composure.

'I've got all the towels I can possibly use. As for the "everything", come on in and close the door, and we'll discuss it.'

She felt her face flushing. 'I'd rather leave it open, thanks.'

He looked up from the open suitcase on the end of the bed and murmured, 'You can trust me. Remember? I'm a preacher's kid.'

'That's got nothing to do with it. I wanted to talk to you about this ridiculous——'

'To say nothing of the fact that Olivia's put me in a room with twin beds. I see I was right last night about her not being precisely liberal in her views——'

'After last night,' Sara interrupted firmly, 'I'm not sure that I——'

'Now, wait a minute. Just what happened last night? I kissed you, for heaven's sake, that's all. A simple kiss, which you invited and participated in.'

'What do you mean, I invited it? I did no such thing!'

'Well, at least you're not denying that you participated.'

She bit her lip. 'No,' she said. 'Not exactly.'

'Good. Because if you told me that you didn't like that kiss, I'd have to go check myself into a padded room next door to Ernie, and I'm enjoying myself far too much to do that.' He took a stack of shirts out of the suitcase and walked across to put them on the shelf of the antique wardrobe. 'And if you expect me to apologise, I'm afraid you'll be disappointed. I don't say I'm sorry for things unless I regret having done them— and the fact is, I'd like to kiss you again, right now.'

He is incorrigible, Sara thought. And, what was

more, it should have been obvious to her that morning at the college that the more fuss she made about it the more intrigued he was going to be. Apparently, the only answer was to stop making a fuss. She shrugged. 'I'm flattered, of course. But please don't repeat the mistake.'

He folded his arms on the back of a chair beside the fireplace. There was an interested gleam in those odd-coloured eyes. 'Why not? Because you liked it too much for comfort?'

'Hardly,' she said stiffly.

Adam grinned. 'You wouldn't care to prove that, would you?' he invited softly. He came across the room to her.

Sara darted a glance toward the door; she had foolishly let him come between her and escape. She could scream, of course, but that would upset Olivia no end.

Adam reached for the suitcase on the floor at her feet and set it on the other twin bed. He had efficiently unpacked half of it before Sara felt she could trust her voice again. You idiot, she told herself. You're jumping at shadows! Just pretend the whole thing never happened, and go back to treating him the way you did before.

'Is there a picture of Pamela anywhere in the house?' he asked suddenly.

'Not that I've ever seen.' She watched as he took a ceramic mug full of pens and pencils out of a plastic bag and set it on the corner of the small desk. The mug was chipped and battered, as if it had been carried around the world.

'Not even in Olivia's room?'

'And just what excuse would you have for being in Olivia's room?' she asked tartly. 'Surely you're going to stop fooling around with the thing about Pamela, aren't you, now that you're living here? Out of courtesy to your hostess, Adam——'

'The rules of etiquette say that a guest should do whatever he can to make his hostess's life more pleasant, and if that means solving her mystery——'

'It could get a little nasty,' Sara pointed out, 'if a skeleton falls out of a closet that you're not supposed to be poking around in.'

He frowned. 'I see your point. All right, I'll think about it, Sara.'

She supposed she would have to be content with that. He took a silver picture frame from the suitcase and set it on the corner of the desk. 'There,' he said. 'That makes it begin to feel like home.'

She had caught just a glimpse of the photograph, of a smiling family. I'm amazed that it isn't a glamorous solo portrait of a lady wearing feathers, she thought. Or a police evidence shot of a bleeding corpse—either of those would seem to be much more likely than a family photo to get a spot on Adam's desk! 'Do you carry around everything you possess?'

'No, but I travel a lot. A few familiar things make a great deal of difference.'

Sara let out a gleeful shriek. 'Things like this?' She pounced on a small, fuzzy item in the bottom corner of the suitcase and held it up.

'Sara, that is personal property!'

'I should say it's personal. So you're human, after all,' she announced, fighting off a case of the giggles. She collapsed into a chair and held the small stuffed dog out at arm's length. 'Do you have to cuddle up with him to get to sleep after you write all that nonsense about torture and mayhem?'

Adam sighed. 'No, I'm not troubled with insomnia,

and I don't cuddle him as I go to sleep. Though, if you're offering your services as a substitute, I'm sure I could get used to cuddling you.'

Sara ignored him. 'Do you know what a gossip column item this would make?' she jeered. 'Famous macho author travels with stuffed dog. What's his name?'

'Buddy.' He looked a bit put out, she thought, as if he'd like to grab the animal back from her and hide it. No wonder, she thought. How perfectly embarrassing for him to be caught with a childhood toy.

'Oh, I see now,' she said. 'It's sewn on his collar. I suppose you got him when you were a baby.'

'I've always had him.'

'He's practically antique.'

'Thanks,' Adam said drily.

'And he's almost worn out, too.' She inspected the dog. His ears flopped disreputably over his face. One beady eye had been replaced by a button, and his tail looked as if it had been chewed. His stuffing had shifted here and there, leaving one of Buddy's front legs too limp to hold his weight. When Sara set him down on the bed, he toppled over with his nose resting against the dark blue bedspread.

She picked him up again and put him on a shelf above the desk, propping him securely between two books. 'There,' she said. 'He can keep you company while you work, and guard you while you sleep.'

Adam was watching her thoughtfully, his arms folded across his chest. 'At least he seems to have restored your good mood.'

'Of course,' Sara said cheerfully. 'Haven't you figured that out? It makes us even, you see—now I've got blackmail material, too!'

*   *   *

Olivia asked Adam to take the head of the table when they went in to dinner, and Sara sighed. That was just what he needed, she thought, for Olivia to start treating him as if he was a permanent resident. She was astounded when Adam refused, with a smile. 'I can't,' he said easily. 'I'm afraid Phillip would haunt me.'

'Phillip,' Olivia said with a sniff. 'Phillip doesn't know which end of my table is the head.'

'He could learn,' Sara put in gently. She didn't like the idea of sticking up for Phillip but, on the other hand, it wasn't fair of Olivia to criticise the man for feeling out of place at Ashton Court when she hadn't made any effort to include him.

She caught Adam looking at her with a speculative light in his eyes. 'Are you certain you aren't hiding something?' he murmured as he held her chair. 'Perhaps you and Phillip are in cahoots, after all.'

She didn't bother to answer. In fact, she didn't take much part in the conversation at all, preferring to listen to the other two. Finally, over dessert, Adam caught her eye across the table. 'You've been awfully quiet,' he accused. 'Are you plotting something?'

'No.' She savoured a bite of peppermint ice-cream and said, 'I've just been wondering why you don't have a Virginia drawl.'

His forehead wrinkled. 'Did I tell you I'd lived there?'

It irritated her. 'You're the most purposely mysterious soul I've ever met, Adam Merrill,' she accused.

'You should know how it feels,' he murmured.

'I'm sure you said you come from Virginia.'

'My parents moved there several years ago,' he corrected. 'Well after I was on my own, I'm afraid—sorry if it disappoints you. My father was offered a church not far from the little town where my mother grew up, and since my grandmother was ill at the time, they wanted to be closer to her. Anything else you'd like to know? We could make a swap of it—I've a few questions myself.'

'Your grandmother must be very proud of you,' Olivia said wistfully.

Adam gave her a smile. 'Oh, she wishes I'd write something she could brag about at her book club, but——'

'Don't we all?' Sara murmured.

'And you, Adam?' Olivia asked. 'Where do you live?'

'I'm sort of a vagabond, Olivia,' he said. 'I find that life's easier when you can just pick up and move on.'

'And he can certainly do that,' Sara said. 'He has all the comforts of home, in one small package.'

Adam flashed a warning look at her. She smiled sweetly at him and subsided. But she thought about it as she finished her dessert. Had he been warning Olivia not to grow to count on him?

Strange, Sara thought. Just a couple of hours ago I thought he might be planning to stay for ever, and I was trying to think of a way to get rid of him. Now I'm just hoping that Olivia won't be hurt when he leaves. She's right—he's charming. Too darned charming . . .

The big walnut-panelled library was the most comfortable place in Ashton Court, Sara had often thought, especially in a summer twilight, when the lamps cast pools of golden light and the last rays of sunlight still made the leaded windows glow. Inside, only the click of Olivia's knitting needles broke the pleasant silence. Companionable, that was what it was, Sara thought as she looked up from her book. Even Adam seemed to be a comfortable part of the scene tonight. He had taken a chair beside the fireplace, across from Olivia's. A notebook lay open on his knee, and now and then he jotted down a word or two. At the moment, it looked as if he was thoughtfully studying the oil portrait of Olivia above the mantel, but Sara thought there was a good chance he wasn't seeing it at all. No doubt he was envisiaging some creepy crime scene instead. It gave her the shivers even to think about it; what kind of mind did a man have to possess in order to write about things like that?

'You're looking very thoughtful, Sara,' Olivia said quietly. 'Is that your new poetry collection you're reading?'

Sara jumped and dropped her book. It bounced once on the carpet and landed at Adam's feet. 'Yes—it's interesting.'

'It doesn't look it,' Adam said mildly. 'You haven't turned a page in five minutes.' He reached for the book and opened it at random.

'I've been thinking about the poems,' she retorted. 'It's not the kind of thing you can speed-read. I'm not certain yet if I believe it's really good and lasting poetry, but——'

'I'm sure,' Adam said. 'It's not.' He tossed the book at her.

'Just because it doesn't rhyme——'

'You don't like poetry that rhymes? Here I am knocking myself out to finish my limerick, and my audience doesn't even appreciate rhyme.'

'I do,' Olivia said brightly. 'Will you read it to me?'

'Please, Olivia, don't encourage him.'

'But I'd like to hear it.'

'Well, I don't plan to listen.'

Adam struck a pose. " 'There was a professor named Prentiss, who said to her good friend the dentist——'' '

'That isn't even a true rhyme,' Sara objected.

'I thought you weren't going to listen. I have a

problem, though—the only rhyme I can think of for my
last line is ''Seventh Day Adventist'' and that doesn't
work into my original idea at all.'

Sara stared at him for a long moment. 'Go back to
writing mysteries,' she recommended.

'I can't believe it, Olivia. She finally said something
good about my books! At last, I think that was a
compliment.'

'Yes,' Sara said with deadly charm, 'it was. They
can't possibly be any worse than that limerick.'

'All right,' he said cheerfully. 'How about, ''There
was a young lady named Sara——'' ' He paused, and
frowned. 'This isn't going to be any easier, I'm afraid.'

'Personally, I still like the old things better,' Olivia
said over the rhythmic click of her needles. 'Elizabeth
Barrett Browning—now, there was a poet. It seems to
me that it takes more talent to make things rhyme than
just to write down words.'

'Not necessarily,' Sara pointed out. 'There's Adam's
limericks, for example, which show no talent at all——'

'But then,' Olivia said comfortably, 'I never really had
time to learn about modern poetry.'

'I'm amazed that Sara reads it,' Adam mused. 'She
seems to think the world took a turn for the worse
when the first novel came out. What do you read,
anyway, Sara, my dear? Surely not poetry all the time.'

'I suppose you think it's silly to enjoy the classics,
too.'

'Do you know what a classic is? It's a book people
praise but never read.'

'You stole that from Mark Twain.'

'Oh, did he agree with me?' Adam asked innocently.
'It's nice to be in good company.'

'I think you would enjoy Adam's books,' Olivia said.
'My copies are all up in my bedroom, but I'll be happy

to loan them to you.'

'Adam doesn't like it when you loan books, Olivia. It cheats him out of royalties.'

'Don't put yourself to any bother, Olivia,' Adam added. 'I'll even give her a copy, so she's got no excuse for not reading it.'

'Autographed?' Sara breathed, in the best imitation of a star-struck fan that she could muster.

'Would you like to have it autographed?'

'Of course. And make it a hard-cover, please. It will be worth more that way.'

'Sara!' Olivia sounded shocked.

'Tell you what,' he said. 'Read it and give me a review, and then I'll autograph it.'

'I'll think it over and let you know if I want to make a deal. But don't hold your breath.' She opened the volume of poetry again and buried her face in it.

A little later Adam laid his notebook aside and excused himself to go make his once-a-week phone call to his mother.

Olivia beamed. 'Isn't that sweet?' she said to Sara, after he'd gone.

'Not necessarily.' Sara didn't look up from her book. 'It's probably the only way she knows where to find him so she can forward his mail.'

Olivia frowned. 'It isn't like you to be cynical, dear.'

Sara was a bit ashamed of herself, both for feeling jealous and for letting it show. She couldn't help thinking of that silver-framed photograph on his desk. It was an attractive family—two very pretty young women, a couple probably in their mid-fifties, and Adam . . . They had looked like they were having a wonderful time.

It brought back all the sense of loss she had felt when her grandmother had died, and later, when her hopes of building a family some day with Guy had been so harshly shattered.

She told herself sternly not to give in to self-pity, and she turned with determination back to her poetry. It didn't help much, and a few minutes later she laid it aside and told Olivia she was going upstairs to do some work.

When Sara went up to her room, there was a book propped conspicuously up on her pillow. She glared at it, remembering how innocently Adam had excused himself from the library. But she certainly hadn't expected him to invade her bedroom.

She picked up the volume; it had a purple and silver dust jacket, and it was called *But Once A Man May Die*. She gulped and put it out of sight behind her night-table. If he thought she was actually going to read it, she decided, he had gone stark, staring crazy!

CHAPTER SIX

A WARM breeze, touched witht the scent of roses, ruffled the stack of papers on the glass-topped patio table, and the fringe on the umbrella above Sara's head rippled rhythmically. She pushed her glasses back up on her nose and reached without enthusiasm for the next essay. It was Sunday, and she could think of a lot of things she'd rather be doing on this pleasant afternoon than reading student papers. But if she let this paperwork build up, she'd never catch up.

Summer classes were always more intense than ones during the regular semester; since there was not the sheer luxury of time, assignments were crammed together, for both students and teachers. And writing classes were particularly difficult, Sara reflected. Two essays a week from each of thirty students equalled an instructor with a migraine headache by the end of the summer session. At least, she reminded herself, it did if the instructor took her responsibilities seriously. Which was more than could be said of a certain other teacher on the block, she thought mutinously, staring across the patio at Adam, who was apparently asleep in a lounge chair.

In a week and a half of classes, she had seen him with a stack of papers precisely once—that first day, when he'd asked his students to write about why they were taking his seminar. Since then, he had managed to implement a pain-free way to teach by having his students read aloud and criticise each other's work. The damnable thing about it, Sara thought, was that the students not only loved it, but their work was steadily getting better as well. She'd found herself caught up in a short story just yesterday—one that was good enough, she thought, to grace any of the national magazines.

Adam is just lucky, she thought. He's got a group of highly motivated students and, fortunately for us all, they're busily teaching themselves to write!

She half turned in her chair to survey him through narrowed eyes. He was stretched out in the lounge chair with a straw hat tilted over his face. He was wearing brief shorts, and his shirt was open to the waist to display a very nicely tanned chest. He looked as if he was prepared to lie there in the sun all afternoon, accomplishing exactly nothing . . .

'Actually,' he said lazily, 'in case you're wondering, I'm working very hard at the moment.'

'At what? Finding excuses not to get up?'

'No. I'm developing the plot of my new book.'

'Of course you are,' she said tartly.

He sat up. 'Weren't you going to accuse me of never doing anything worth while? As a matter of fact, I work most of the time. It just doesn't always show.'

'I've heard that tune before.' She turned back to her stack of papers and didn't see the quizzical light in his eyes.

Thank heaven, Sara thought, that I won't be teaching at all during the second summer session. Five whole weeks to lie in the sun and enjoy myself. Perhaps I will actually have time to read something for fun.

'Really? Who told you?'

'What?' She realised what he was asking, and coloured a bit. 'It's nothing important. I just used to know someone who wrote, that's all. He would work for a week sometimes, crafting a sentence, and then throw it out.'

Adam said, wisely, 'Not a commercially successful writer, I see.'

She laughed, unwillingly. That was an understatement, when it came to Guy, she thought. One brilliant short novel, and then nothing, ever again. I wonder, she thought, if Guy wrote that first book himself, or if it was actually someone else's work. A student's, perhaps. It was the first time the possibility had occurred to her.

'Are we talking about the man in your life? It's not very thoughtful of him to call himself a writer—it gives the rest of us a bad name.' He studied her thoughtfully through narrowed eyes and added, 'Perhaps I shouldn't be taking this personally, Sara, but is that why you're so touchy whenever I come near you?'

Am I still being touchy? she wondered. She hadn't thought so; for the last week, since he had moved into Ashton Court, Adam hadn't even tried to get close, and he certainly had made no move to kiss her again. He had teased and tormented her unmercifully, of course, but there was nothing personal in that. He teased and tormented Olivia, too.

She shrugged it off. 'It would explain it, wouldn't it?'

'Not to my satisfaction,' Adam said cheerfully. 'He's him. I'm me. It's really not fair of you to compare us.'

'The critics would probably agree,' Sara murmured.

'I may not be literary, but I'm an honest-to-goodness writer. I don't spend a week on a single sentence, because I can't afford to.'

'But you can obviously afford to spend a summer lying on the patio.'

'That's different,' he pointed out. 'It's not my money I'm spending this summer—it's Olivia's.'

'And you haven't touched your typewriter since you

ROMANCE READERS!

Take 4 Free books and 2 Free gifts with <u>NO</u> obligation

In each spellbinding Mills & Boon Romance you'll discover a world filled with enthralling plots, characters you can relate to and above all - love, passion, and excitement. A world that you can share!

And as a special introductory offer we'll send you 4 specially selected Romances and 2 glass dishes plus a surprise mystery gift Absolutely Free when you complete and return this card.

We'll also reserve a subscription for you to our Reader Service, which means you could enjoy:-

- 🌹 **6 BRAND NEW ROMANCES -** sent direct to you every month before they're available in the shops.
- 🌹 **FREE POSTAGE AND PACKING -** there are no hidden costs.
- 🌹 **FREE MONTHLY NEWSLETTER -** packed with author news, competitions, special subscriber offers and much, much more.
- 🌹 **SPECIAL OFFERS -** Bargain book offers just for subscribers.

CLAIM YOUR FREE GIFTS OVERLEAF

Mills & Boon
FREEPOST
P.O. Box 236
Croydon
CR9 9EL

FREE BOOKS CERTIFICATE

FREE GIFT

Yes! Please send me my 4 Free **romances** together with my 2 **glass dishes and surprise mystery gift.** Please also reserve a special Reader Service Subscription for me. If I decide to subscribe, I shall receive 6 Brand New Romances every month for just £7.50 post and packing free. If I decide not to subscribe I shall write to you within 10 days. The free books and gifts will be mine to keep in any case. I understand that I am under no obligation whatsoever - I can cancel or suspend my subscription at any time simply by writing to you.. *I am over 18 years of age*

1A9R

Return this card now and we'll also send you this 2 piece glass dish absolutely Free together with....

A SURPRISE MYSTERY GIFT.

We all love surprises, so as well as the FREE books and glass dishes, there's an intriguing mystery gift especially for you.

POST TODAY!

NAME _____

ADDRESS _____

_____

_____

POSTCODE _____

unpacked it.'

'Thinking is a lot more important than typing, most of the time. Besides, how would you know? The walls are too thick to eavesdrop. Have you been searching my waste-basket when I go out?'

'No, but I've been taking a lot of messages from your agent, who certainly believes that you aren't doing a bit of work.'

'He didn't want me to come out here this summer.'

'I can see why.'

'I can't. He knows perfectly well I'll start writing again in September, because I always do. And I've never missed a deadline.'

'Well, I wish you'd tell him to stop calling, or I'm going to have to buy a special spindle just for your stacks of messages.'

'Do you know, I believe you're changing the subject, Sara, my dear. You haven't answered my question, you know. Is the gent who's so careful with his words the former love of your life?'

Did the man never let go of an idea? 'Yes,' she said crisply. 'Does that satisfy you?'

'Not as much as some other things you could say to me, if you were in the right frame of mind,' he mused.

Bandying words with a writer is a losing battle, Sara told herself. She put her glasses back on and turned to her stack of papers.

'But of course I'm glad that he's only your *former* love,' Adam mused. 'It quite gives me hope.'

'Would you stop?' she demanded without looking up.

'Only if you'll come and play a set of tennis with me.'

'Can't.'

'There's a racquet in the back hall closet, and I'll bet a dollar it doesn't belong to Olivia.'

'I didn't say I don't play. I said I'm too busy.'

'I'll help you with your papers tonight if you'll come and play tennis with me this afternoon,' he bargained.

She looked up in astonishment. 'You? You're actually volunteering to work?'

He looked at the stack with a jaundiced eye, but said firmly, 'That's me. Always willing to help. You work too hard, you know. You didn't even take Saturday night off——'

Olivia came out on to the terrace, every hair precisely in place. Her pink linen suit was a masterpiece of tailoring, and a tiny matching hat with a single feather was perched over one ear. 'Oh, here you are,' she said vaguely. 'I did remember to tell you, didn't I, that I'm going to a bridge party this afternoon?'

'No,' Sara murmured. 'You didn't.'

'And then——' Olivia's cheeks coloured a little, or perhaps it was just the reflection of sunlight against her suit as she moved '—I'm going on to cocktails and dinner at the Talbots' house, and afterwards Simon may stop by for a while and play cribbage, so if you two have other things you'd like to do——'

'We're going to play tennis,' Adam said.

Olivia gave him a sunny smile. 'What a lovely idea, dear.' She tripped off toward the garage.

A moment later, Adam said thoughtfully, 'I see what you mean about her sending the children out to play. You don't believe she's serious about Simon, do you?'

'Why do you ask?' Sara said gently. 'Were you already planning what you could do with Ashton Court? Phillip's ahead of you—he's scheming to turn it into condos.'

'It would never work.'

'Simon and Olivia?'

'No, Ashton Court cut into condos. But that's the sort

of criminality I'd expect from Phillip—petty, foolish, and doomed to failure. Change your clothes and get your racquet.'

He seemed to be taking for granted that she had accepted the invitation. 'All right, I'll go,' she said. 'But remember, you promised to help with the paperwork tonight.'

She ran upstairs to change into tennis shorts, and found Annabelle in the sitting-room of her suite, freshening an arrangement of flowers. 'I thought you'd gone home,' Sara said. 'It's supposed to be your day off, anyway.'

'These flowers needed doing. I've left a cold supper in the refrigerator for you and Mr Merrill.'

'Thanks, Annabelle.' Sara went on into her bedroom and paused at the sight of a purple and silver book lying on the love-seat.

'Oh, in case you've been looking for your book,' the housekeeper called, 'I found it behind your night-table. It must have fallen back there.'

'Thanks,' Sara said crisply. Well, at least it hadn't crawled up there by itself, she thought. Was everyone getting into the conspiracy? The damned book would probably turn up in the shower next!

They walked the few blocks to the country club; it was silly, Sara announced, to drive somewhere for the purpose of taking exercise. Two fast-paced sets of tennis later, she was breathlessly beginning to regret that she would have to walk home. Adam had a wicked backhand, and she had chased it all over the court until she was about to drop.

'I'll buy you a cold drink,' she offered as they came up the slope from the tennis courts to the clubhouse.

'As an award for winning?'

'No,' she admitted. 'Because I can't make it home

without one. I'm out of shape!'

His eyes roved gently over her body, assessing her trim shorts, low-necked shirt, and blonde hair tucked up under a visored cap. 'Oh, I wouldn't say that,' he mused.

Colour burned furiously up her throat and splashed across her cheeks. She turned away, trying to ignore his chuckle, and stumbled into Phillip, who was just coming out of the pro shop.

He caught her and recoiled. 'You're all wet, Sara. And you look as if you're about to have a coronary. What have you been doing?' Then he saw Adam behind her and added, 'Who's minding Olivia, if I may ask?'

'You know, I think we should talk about that, Phillip,' Adam said smoothly. 'Come along and have a drink with us.'

Phillip blinked warily, as if he sensed a trap somewhere, and finally nodded.

Sara was a bit shocked herself, both at the invitation and the response, and she rolled her eyes at Adam, making frantic questioning motions behind Phillip's back as they walked across the lounge. Adam just raised his eyebrows at her, as if he didn't understand.

Phillip paused to greet a man at the bar. Adam guided Sara to an isolated corner table and, as he held her chair, she said under her breath, 'Why on earth did you let us in for this?'

'Sara, it ought to be clear to anyone with the intelligence of a golf ball why I did it. You said you'd ask him exactly when Pamela disappeared.'

'I haven't had a chance!'

'So I've got you one.'

'I thought you'd given that project up, anyway,' Sara muttered. 'You haven't said anything about it in days——'

He glared her into silence and then leaned back in his chair and smiled angelically at Phillip. 'What will it be, Phil? I'll go get the drinks and save the waitress the trouble of coming over.'

The look he directed at Sara made it clear that he was in no mood to accept excuses. She shredded a paper napkin in her lap and stared at the fragments. There was no tactful way to ask, she decided. She would just have to plunge in and hope that Phillip wasn't in a curious frame of mind himself.

'How is Olivia enjoying having a tame rabbit around the house?' Phillip asked. He jerked his head toward Adam.

'Tame rabbit?' Sara asked weakly. There was nothing less like a tame rabbit than Adam Merrill, she thought. She could see him cast as a snake, perhaps, or as a cat, graceful and charming and self-centred—but a rabbit? Never.

'I ask you, Sara—is this any way for a sensible woman to act? Now she's got two free-loaders living with her——

'Thank you,' Sara said crisply.

'Sorry if it hurts your feelings, but you must admit it's true of you, too. Sometimes I wonder if the woman has all her mental faculties. This whole idea she's got that Pamela isn't actually dead——'

Sara breathed a sigh of relief. At least he'd given her an opening, so she didn't have to bring the subject up herself. 'She could be alive, you know,' she pointed out. 'She was only twenty or so when she disappeared.'

'But it's been forty years——'

'Exactly forty? Are you certain?'

He glared at her suspiciously. 'Why are you so

interested?'

Sara shrugged. 'I was just figuring out the other day how old Olivia must be, and it just doesn't seem possible that it could be forty years since Pamela vanished. Wasn't Olivia past thirty when Pamela was born?' Not a bad story, she congratulated herself, for the spur of the moment.

Phillip frowned. 'Well, maybe it wasn't quite that long,' he said finally. 'Thirty-five years ago, perhaps. I don't see that it matters much whether it was five years one way or the other.'

Not to you, maybe, Sara thought. But it may have saved me from a nasty lecture!

Adam came back with a tray. 'An iced tea,' he said, setting it in front of Sara, 'and a bourbon and soda for you, Phil, and a nice cold beer for me. You don't mind me coming back, do you? I thought, the way you had your heads together over here, you might have been discussing something private.'

Sara could have cheerfully sliced him to ribbons.

'You said you wanted to talk to me about Olivia,' Phillip reminded.

Trust Phillip, she thought. He could be a bulldog at times, and if he wasn't distracted from the subject it could get nasty. 'Phillip,' she said quickly. 'I've been thinking, and——'

He brightened. 'About my idea?' he said quickly. 'The two of us? It would solve the problem.'

It took a moment for her to remember what he was talking about; so much had happened to her since his half-proposal of marriage. She caught Adam's eye across the table; his violet-blue gaze held more than a touch of irony.

'Not exactly,' she began. 'I mean, I'm not sure I'm ready to think about marriage——'

'About Olivia,' Adam interrupted. 'She's getting forgetful.'

Sara stared at him with her mouth open. She was glad he'd rescued her, but whose side was he on, anyway? Of course, he hadn't heard Phillip's earlier comment about Olivia's mental state, but couldn't he see the danger in giving the man any information at all? If Phillip had his way, Olivia would find herself in a strait-jacket one of these days—if that was what it took for her nephew to get his hands on Ashton Court.

'How do you mean, forgetful?' Phillip asked slyly.

'Oh, nothing that's actually dangerous to her,' Adam said smoothly. 'Today she remembered that she was going out with her friends, but she forgot that she hadn't told Sara about it. But of course she shouldn't be living on her own, and as for driving herself around this town in her car——'

'That's been bothering me, too,' Phillip said. 'She might forget where she is, and hurt herself.'

Well done, Phillip, Sara thought. Just the right tone of nervous anxiety.

Phillip hitched himself forward in his chair and waved his swizzle stick. 'But what can I do about it? She won't listen to me.'

'I think a bit of firmness is all that's needed, actually,' Adam confided. 'All this talk of hers about having a man around the house—Olivia really wants to be told what to do, you see. The more you ask and plead, the more determined she's going to be. But if you were to go in and say, "This is the way things have to be, Aunt Olivia——" '

Olivia will kill him on the spot if he dares to do anything so ridiculous, Sara thought. She'll certainly phone her solicitor immediately and take him out of the will—if he's in it at all . . .

Which would leave the field wide open for someone else, she thought. Like Adam. She had teased him about it before, but she hadn't taken the possibility really seriously. Now she began to wonder in earnest if Adam Merrill fancied the idea of owning Ashton Court.

When Phillip rose to leave a few minutes later, he paused beside Sara's chair and said, a bit uncomfortably, 'Perhaps—about that other matter, Sara—you know, the suggestion I made? I think we'd better just wait a while, and see . . .'

'Certainly,' she said gravely. 'Let me know if you change your mind, Phillip.'

Adam watched Phillip leave the room, and then turned sombre eyes on Sara. 'I think you've been jilted,' he announced. 'Phillip has decided he can have it all——'

'And it's all your fault, too.' She put her hand to her head, feigning distraction. 'If you hadn't interrupted with all that stuff and Olivia, he might have actually said the words.'

'Which words?'

'You know—will you marry me?'

He grinned. 'I'll think about it; thanks for asking. It feels a bit funny, though; I always thought that when it came my time I'd be the one to pop the question.'

Sara closed her eyes, bit her tongue and decided to be silent till he was done.

'Besides,' he went on, 'if you won't even let me kiss you, how do you expect me to know if I'd like to marry you? There are limits to my mind-reading capacity, you know, and if you remain so stand-offish——'

Her good intentions evaporated. 'I'm not stand-offish. And I certainly didn't say that I wanted to marry you.'

He looked astonished. 'Surely you're not suggesting

some sort of immoral arrangement instead? My father would be shocked, Sara.'

She glared at him. 'I've a feeling that there's not a great deal left that could shock your father, Adam Merrill. After all, he survived raising you!'

'Your point, I think,' he murmured. He picked up her hand and put a quick kiss on the back of it. 'Shall we go home now, or stay and see if we can gather a crowd for a repeat performance? The lady in black over there looks quite intrigued, for instance.'

The evening was warm and still. The scent of steaks on barbecue grills drifted along the street, along with the sounds of children playing in the gathering twilight. On the campus of Chandler College, lights poured through the tall arched doors of the library and glowed from the windows of the dormitory complex. 'I'd never thought about it before,' Sara mused, 'but I wonder—which room was Pamela's?' She waved a hand up at the red-brick bulk of the building.

'You're sure that's where she lived?'

Sara nodded. 'That's the only girls' dormitory which was here that long ago.'

'She sounds like the sorority type, somehow.'

'Oh, I don't know. Don't you think that's where her contrariness came in? Her parents would have wanted her to join a sorority, so of course she wouldn't do it.'

'I suppose so.' He sounded dissatisfied. 'Did you find anything out from Phillip?'

'Not much. He decided it might have been five years earlier or later—it didn't seem to matter to him.'

'I don't suppose it would.'

They walked on in silence for another block. 'It's really got you, hasn't it?' Sara said. 'I honestly thought you'd given it up, you know.'

'Give up the whole Pamela problem?' His smile

flashed. 'It's too good a title to waste.'

Sara considered that and shook her head. 'I don't think it would sell,' she said. 'Not enough death and violence for your readers.'

'I wouldn't say that.'

'Adam—you think she's dead, don't you?'

He didn't answer for a long time. 'It's the only logical answer, don't you think? Even big family feuds usually die out after a few years. If she is out there, wouldn't she have come to understand by now that this kind of adolescent squabble happens between every child and her parents? She could have children of her own—grandchildren, even—and she would know by now from her own experience how much it hurts when a child rejects her parents.'

'Perhaps she was afraid to come back, to face up to it,' Sara said softly. 'Sometimes fear keeps us prisoner, and won't let us do the things we know we should.'

He reached for her hand then, and they walked along with fingers clasped, in silence.

'What about you, Sara?' he asked finally.

'I don't understand.'

'Is it fear that keeps you here, that keeps you alone? You can't convince me that Olivia discourages you from dating——'

'Oh, no.' Her tone was dry. 'When I first moved into Ashton Court, I came home an average of once a week to find Olivia taking tea with a young man. Coincidentally, she always had to go and refill the kettle the moment I walked in, so I found myself entertaining the visitor. Well, that simply had to stop.'

'Because you didn't like the attention?'

'Because Olivia detests tea,' Sara said firmly. 'I finally persuaded her to stop martyring herself, and convinced her that I was not interested in dating anyone. It's been much more peaceful around the house ever since.'

The silence dragged on until they were almost to the gates of Ashton Court. 'What is it,' he asked finally, 'that makes you prefer stone-cold solitude, Sara?'

She intended to ignore the question and to turn the conversation in some other, easier direction. But, before she could find a quip, he said, 'I wish I understood. He must have been an Olympic-sized rat, but still——'

It was matter-of-fact, but Sara found tears stinging her eyes. 'Yes, he was,' she whispered.

And then, to her own amazement, she heard herself telling him about Guy. Not all the details; she could never share those with anyone. But she told him of how lonely she had been that year, after her grandmother had died, and how Guy had filled that gap for her. She told him of her faith in Guy, and how she had worked so hard for their future together, and how it had felt the day she had seen him with his wife, and known that everything she had believed in had been only a lie . . .

'So you see, loving someone just wasn't worth it for me,' she finished. 'I'm better off alone.'

'I don't see,' Adam objected. 'You were lonely, and the louse knew that, and used it for his own selfish purposes. But how you've managed to convince yourself that there isn't anything better in the world——'

'It just hurt too much, that's how I know.'

'Living hurts, Sara, if you're doing it right. You can't wander through life avoiding every ache and pain, or you might as well be dead!'

'You don't understand.'

'You might be surprised. We all have injuries, Sara. But if we let our fear shut us away from other people——' He sounded tired and disillusioned.

'What about you, Adam?' she whispered.

For a long moment, she thought he wasn't going to

answer. He opened the wrought-iron gate, and they walked up the driveway towards the house. He swung his tennis racquet viciously at an invisible lob, and said, 'There was a girl once. But both her parents could trace their family trees back to the Mayflower and a whole long ways beyond, while I——'

'You were just the preacher's kid,' she finished.

He looked down at her then, and after a long moment he said, 'Yeah.'

'But that's ridiculous, Adam. What matters is what you are, not what some ancestor did, centuries ago!'

He stopped and turned to face her. 'Sometimes, to some people, it seems to matter a great deal.'

She looked up at him for a long moment in the fading twilight, as if she expected someone else to have suddenly appeared beside her, instead of him. Humorous flippancy had been such a large part of him that this sudden seriousness had come as a shock. 'Adam——' she said uncertainly, and laid a slender hand against his chest. 'Not to me. It doesn't matter to me.'

He drew a short, sharp breath, and pulled her close. His mouth was warm and firm and strong against hers, and Sara closed her eyes and waited for that inevitable panic to strike her, the moment when the arms that cradled her would become a sort of prison, when the mouth that caressed her would turn into a smothering mask.

It didn't happen. Instead, a tiny bubble of warmth seemed to come to life inside her, rising and expanding until she seemed to be floating in his arms. She pressed herself against him, frantically seeking to stay there beside him, knowing that if she let that bubble burst nothing would ever be the same again, and yet not caring what might happen after that——

When he moved to release her, she uttered a little

groan of protest, and he laughed breathlessly and pulled her close again. 'Sara, my dear, it was only words, wasn't it? You can't really believe that being alone is better than this. And if this is an invitation to make love to you, I'd be delighted to accept it. But shouldn't we go inside first?'

The universe seemed to grind to a harsh, shuddering halt for an instant. What have I done? she thought grimly. I'm standing on the front lawn of Ashton Court, kissing him like a lover.

She had thought that the passionate side of her nature had died that day when her love for Guy had withered into dust. In the years since she had left him, she had not been tempted to look for physical fulfilment in the arms of another man.

Now, in the space of a few minutes, with the gentleness of a caress, Adam had forced her to admit that she was a woman who had known love, and who now missed it.

The physical side of love had not been exactly earthshaking for Sara, but it had been enjoyable, none the less. In the last few years, she had deliberately closed off that part of her nature and told herself that the pleasure to be found in intimacy was not worth the risk. And she had succeeded in making herself believe it, until Adam's persistent presence had worn down the wall she had built.

That was all this attraction to Adam was, she told herself: the natural longings of a woman's nature, a woman who for years had tried to ignore her physical needs. It was no wonder that it had happened; he was an unconscionably good-looking man who made no secret of the fact that he would like to make love to her. Any woman could be pardoned for considering the possibility, but it certainly didn't mean she was ready to hop into bed with him.

She told him that, briefly and mechanically.

He listened politely, kissed the bridge of her nose, and said, 'I'd believe you more easily, you know, if you weren't still snuggled up against me while you're turning me down.'

Sara uttered a furious little scream as she realised that she was indeed still in his arms. Adam laughed at her and let her go, but she was uncomfortably aware that he didn't believe she meant it, and he thought that sooner or later she would change her mind.

And the real trouble, she realised, the thing that truly terrified her, was the knowledge that if he had held her just a little longer she might have done just that.

CHAPTER SEVEN

THE THOUGHT of going to bed with him was the most ridiculous idea she had ever contemplated, Sara reminded herself a couple of hours later as she sat at her desk with her red pen suspended above a particularly dreadful student composition.

Of course she was never going to fall in love again. But if she ever should, Sara told herself emphatically, it would be with a man who was trustworthy, solid, dependable—a man with a steady job and a steady life. It certainly would not be with an adventurer—an opportunist like Adam Merrill. He had said himself that he was a vagabond, and that he found life much easier when he could just pick up and move on. How much more clearly could he have said that he didn't intend to be tied down with baggage—emotional, or any other kind?

'Not that I would want him to consider me as his personal possession,' she told herself tartly. 'I'm not just another suitcase to be dragged along on his travels!'

And she would truly be a fool if she had an affair with him on his terms. He'd be at Chandler College for less than a month, and then who knew what would draw his fancy? She wouldn't put it past him to abruptly decide to cross the Atlantic in a rowing-boat! But, no matter where he went, he would go by himself, and she would have nothing left.

Well, not quite. 'I'd have memories,' Sara muttered.

And if he was the kind of lover she suspected he might be—tender and gentle and kind—the memories

111

would probably be very good ones . . .

'Stop it,' she ordered herself. 'You're getting crazy, Sara Prentiss. You ought to know better than even to think about it!'

She turned her attention back to the essay and managed to read two terrible paragraphs of it before her mind skidded off the track again.

She had told him things tonight that she had thought she would never speak of to another human being. And she suspected that she knew things about him that would have surprised even his mother; she could not imagine him talking about the girl whose parents had thought him not good enough for their daughter. How very foolish of them, and how very heartbreaking for a young man in love.

And, quite possibly, how very inaccurate, she thought. He knew precisely how to touch her heart, that was certain. But Guy had told her things like that, too, and they had turned out to be lies. Why should she believe what Adam said?

'Because he's different,' she said aloud, as if the words were forced from her, and then she shook her head in confusion and tossed her pen down. She'd just have to finish the papers some other time; sitting here all night obviously wasn't going to accomplish anything.

She wished for an instant that she had taken Adam up on his offer to help; he had renewed it while they were raiding the refrigerator to see what Annabelle had left there, but her head had still been spinning from the after-effects of his kiss and her own confusion, and so she had politely declined. He hadn't argued about it. He had simply started to talk about other things, but she had known by the amused gleam in his eyes that he had predicted that result. It was probably the only reason he had made the offer, she thought; he certainly hadn't been intrigued by the idea of working!

But it would have been pleasant to spend the evening with him, even if they were both absorbed in work. It would have been a companionable silence, a friendly one, interrupted now and then by a shared look or a phrase read from a student's paper . . .

She quickly found that lying in the darkness was no more apt to bring peace of mind than staring mindlessly at that stack of essays. The air in her room felt warm and stuffy; the breeze of early evening had died, and the curtains were still. Her thin cotton nightshirt felt as heavy as a parka, and after half an hour of tossing restlessly she turned the bedside lamp on and looked for something that would have the capacity to distract her thoughts. The poetry collection wasn't it, she decided; it required too much concentration. She had read all the new issues of her magazines, and it would be foolish to get dressed again to go down to the library after a book—and even more foolish, she thought, to wander around the house in her nightshirt!

Ultimately, she picked up *But Once A Man May Die.* At least then she could honestly tell Olivia that she'd made an effort to read it. It was getting a bit tiresome to be asked about it, as Olivia did at least once a day. Sometimes, Sara thought, she could understand the temptation Pamela must have felt to disagree automatically with anything Olivia said, no matter how reasonably it was phrased!

Besides, with any luck—despite the breathtaking plot promised by the dust-jacket—in half an hour she'd be bored and sleepy and ready to drop off for a peaceful night.

At two o'clock, a sound outside her door made her sit up straight, her heart pounding, before she sternly told herself not to be juvenile, and turned back to the book.

At three, a timber in Ashton Court's roof creaked, and Sara nearly cracked her head on the canopy of the Jacobean bed before she could remind herself that the murderer was confined, after all, between two cardboard covers.

At four, she laid the book aside for a moment, with her index finger holding her place, so she could close her eyes—which were burning as if she'd rubbed an onion over them—for a moment.

And at a quarter-past seven, she roused with a scream when a cold, wet object trailed across her forehead. She shot up in the bed, rigid as a poker, stared straight into Adam's violet-blue eyes, and said, 'Why the hell are you in my bedroom?' She blinked droplets of water out of her eyes. 'I suppose this is the sort of thing you think is funny!'

'I find some humour in it, yes.' He returned the dripping flannel to the bathroom and added, as he came back with a towel, 'Or had you reached the part yet where they find the body tangled in seaweed on the beach?' He dried his hands and threw the towel at her.

'Yes, I have, thank you—I managed to guess that was what you were imitating. You have a juvenile sense of humour, do you know that, Adam Merrill?' She slammed the book down on her bedside-table and mopped her forehead dry.

'And you, Sara, my dear,' he said softly, 'have the sort of body that could incite a man to riot—do you know that?' As if to emphasise his point, his gaze drifted down over the sheer cotton of her nightshirt to rest caressingly on the slim length of her bare legs.

She slid under the covers with a shriek and pulled them almost over her head.

'I'd like to interpret that as an invitation to join you,'

he said, 'but I'm sure you realise we have to be in class in ten minutes.'

She peered out from under the blanket at her bedside clock, and groaned. 'At least that explains why you're here.'

'Though if I'd had any idea how luscious you look against a satin pillow, I'd have found an excuse before now,' he went on relentlessly. 'You can oversleep any day you like, Sara—depend on it, I'll be in to wake you. But next time, would you mind wearing somthing blue and lacy? That's nice enough for a nightshirt, but I have sort of a fancy to see you in——'

'Out!' she shrieked.

'Does that mean you don't need my help to get dressed?' he mocked from the door. 'I must admit that I'd rather finish undressing you, but——'

She picked up *But Once A Man May Die* and flung it at him. It bounced harmlessly off the door just as he pulled it shut behind him.

She made it downstairs in three minutes flat. Without a word he put a mug full of fresh coffee in her hand and ushered her out to the Corvette.

By the time she had finished the coffee, Sara was begining to feel human, and they had reached the classroom. 'I suppose I should thank you for waking me up,' she began.

'Don't bother,' he said with a grin. 'The fact that you adore my work enough to stay up all night reading it is thanks enough.'

It was certainly past time to puncture that self-satisfied air of his, she thought. 'Your precious book put me to sleep,' she retorted, neglecting to mention how long it had taken. 'It was hardly the most exciting thing I've ever read.'

The accusation glanced off him. 'Oh, if that was the

problem,' he murmured, 'you should have taken me to bed with you last night instead of the book. I'll guarantee you wouldn't have gone to sleep then.'

It had got to be a habit for the three of them to gather in the library at Ashton Court after dinner. Sometimes they played cards; more often, each of them pursued a private pastime. It would be even cosier when winter came, Sara thought idly, and they could have a fire. She had constructed quite an elaborate daydream before she remembered that, long before cold weather closed in around Ashton Court, Adam would be gone.

She told herself that the sort of hollow feeling around her heart was only a foolish weakness. Two weeks of his stay were already past. The days were slipping by at what seemed a furious speed, with mornings spent in the classroom and afternoons in her office, where she was finding him far too regularly for her comfort.

When she had asked him to return her key, Adam had announced that it would be heartless of her to expect him to put up with Ernie Ryan's shortcomings on a daily basis. He had been shelling peanuts on her desk blotter when he said it, and Sara had stared thoughtfully at the pile of hulls and wondered just who was having the most frustrating time of it. It was a toss-up between herself and Professor Ryan, she concluded; Adam wasn't even in the running. But short of physical violence there didn't seem to be any way to get her key back, so she had held her tongue and started taking her work home in the afternoons. He was intentionally sabotaging her concentration, she thought. He was always *there*, and every time he looked at her she could see in those incredible eyes the memory of that last kiss, days ago now, but as fresh in her memory as if it had happened just a moment since.

And every time he looked at her, those violet-blue eyes seemed to be asking if she had changed her mind yet . . .

She shivered a little and went to put a record on. The mournful opening phrases of *Rhapsody in Blue* poured into the room.

Adam looked up from his magazine. 'I'd have guessed Bach was more your thing.'

'It is.' Olivia clipped her thread and shook out the dress she was working on. 'She only plays Gershwin because she knows I like him better than the other stuff.'

'I'm not that unselfish, Olivia.' Sara leaned over the back of the old lady's chair to inspect her work. 'It's beautiful, darling.' The dress had been a severely plain champagne-coloured silk when Olivia had found it on the sale rack in a downtown store. It had done wonderful things for Sara's figure and her colouring even then; now, with the addition of an antique tatted-lace collar and matching cuffs, it was becoming a model any designer would have been proud of.

'It's almost done,' Olivia said. She frowned at her needle and put it aside. 'I'll finish tomorrow; it's getting too dark to do such fine work.' She folded the dress and laid it into her work-basket, then picked up a soft mass of sky-blue wool that was rapidly becoming a cable-knit sweater. Her needles began to click placidly against the rising tempo of the music.

'Shouldn't you have a light?' Sara asked.

'To knit? Oh, no. I could do this pattern blindfolded. Would you like a sweater in green, too, Sara?'

'Olivia, you shouldn't——'

'But I'll have plenty of time before winter. And you know that I like you to have pretty things.'

Sara caught a quizzical look in Adam's eyes and was

instantly irritated; was he trying to make her feel guilty? It wasn't as if she asked Olivia to give her things, after all.

She twisted the aquamarine ring on her finger. That was the exception, she thought. It was one thing for Olivia to knit her sweaters and buy her a dress now and then. She brought Olivia gifts, too. But, despite what Olivia had said about the aquamarine being only a trinket, it was obviously a valuable piece of jewellery—far too valuable for Sara to accept.

However, every time she had tried to give it back, Olivia had simply smiled and said again how much it pleased her to see Sara getting such enjoyment from it, and what a sin it would be to keep such a pretty thing locked away in a jewellery case . . .

And it was certainly pretty, Sara thought; that was part of the problem. She found herself growing attached to the gorgeous thing, wearing it more and more often, even when there was no conceivable excuse for such an elaborate piece of jewellery.

She twisted the ring off her finger and stared into the stone, watching the play of light in its clear depths. It wasn't as lively now, under the lamp, as it was in daylight. I wonder, Sara thought, what made her choose to give it to me. Why a ring, in the first place? And why aquamarine, instead of an opal, or a tourmaline? Those are my birthstones——

The light caught on something engraved on the inner surface of the band, and Sara turned it the barest fraction of an inch so she could study it more closely. She opened her mouth to exclaim, and then shut it again firmly. This discovery, she decided, would bear thinking about before she said anything to anyone.

'If you like that tatted collar,' Olivia said, 'I've got some patterns in the attic.'

'Funny, isn't it, how things come back into style every so often?' Sara murmured.

'I haven't tatted in years, but I'm sure I haven't forgotten how. It's just a matter of getting the rhythm, you know. And I have to find something to do with my hands.' Her smile at Adam was fond. 'My favourite author won't have another new book out till Christmas.'

'Please don't complain to the publisher, Olivia,' Adam said lazily. 'They might decide to publish two a year instead of only one, and then I'd have to buckle down and work.'

'I know, but——' Olivia sounded unhappy. 'Perhaps Sara was the wise one, after all, to save them up and read them all at once.'

'That's a thought,' Sara mused. 'If I save the rest till I'm ninety——'

'Did you ever finish the book?' Adam asked. 'I've been waiting all week for you to ask if I'd sit beside you and hold your hand while you read the last chapter.' And after you finished that, his eyes seemed to be saying, there are other things we could do together . . .

'I finished it.'

'Did you like the ending?'

Sara thought his air of anxiety was a performance worthy of an award. 'Not particularly.' Her tone was blighting.

'Good—you weren't supposed to. But you must admit it was effective, wasn't it?'

She was darned if she'd admit that it had been so effective she had slept with her bedside lamp burning the night she had finished the last chapter. 'Your books are like popcorn, Adam.'

'Books?' he questioned innocently. 'Plural?'

'All right, so I read *The Fine Art of Murder*, too. Are

you satisfied?'

'Not entirely. But tell me—what's wrong with popcorn? It's good, it's satisfying, it's not fattening.'

'It doesn't last.'

He grinned. 'But one handful leads to another.'

'So people all over the country are waiting for Christmas, anticipating another Adam Merrill mystery tucked into their stockings? Preserve me.'

'What's the next one called?' Olivia asked.

Too Difficult to Die.'

'I can hardly wait,' Sara muttered.

'Really? I'll get you a copy,' Olivia said brightly. 'I knew, as soon as you'd read one, that you'd be hooked, Sara.'

Adam choked back a laugh at the chagrin in Sara's face. 'Hard cover, of course,' he said gently. 'And I'll autograph it.'

'Would you, dear?' Olivia said mildly. 'I didn't like to ask, since I didn't know where you'd be by Christmas.'

Sara wanted to stand up and cheer. So much for Adam's plans—if he really had any—of staying on permanently at Ashton Court!

'I haven't any idea,' Adam said. It was prompt, with no sign of distress, which completely ruined Sara's fun. 'But I'll give you my address in Chicago; it will always catch up with me, Olivia. And I'll make sure that you have one of the first copies off the press.'

Was there just the slightest emphasis on the *you*? Sara wondered. Well, if he expected her to be upset at Olivia getting favoured treatment, he was wrong.

'That's great,' she said. 'If Adam's going to give you a copy, Olivia, you won't need to buy one at all. I'll borrow yours, if I find that I can't withstand the temptation.'

Olivia ignored her. 'You'll be going to Chicago when

you finish with your class, Adam?'

'I'm not sure what I'll do. Probably I'll go to Virginia for a while. I haven't seen my parents for several months. But I'll be in Chicago on September the first to start the new book—I always am.'

'You're actually superstitious?' Sara asked. 'Isn't that a bit uncomfortable for you? Considering your line of work, I mean.'

'I suppose you could say it's superstition. I can write anywhere, once I'm started. But I always start a new book in Chicago, on the first day of September. It hasn't failed me in six years, so why argue with success?'

'Oh, that reminds me,' Olivia said. 'Would you give me your mother's address, Adam? I want to write to her and tell her how proud she shoud be of her son.'

'Keep it up, Olivia,' Sara advised, 'and you might get two autographed copies!'

'Don't mind her, Adam, she's only jealous,' Olivia said. 'Do you know where I left my other skein of yarn, Sara? I think I can finish this sleeve tonight.'

Sara shook her head. 'I haven't seen it.' She rose and went to flip through the rack of music.

'Perhaps it's in my bedroom.'

'Would you like me to go get it?'

'Thank you, dear, but I haven't any idea where to tell you to look.' Olivia put the mass of wool aside and went out. 'The drawer of my bureau, perhaps?' she was saying under her breath.

A crashing chord rang through the library. Sara hummed along with the first phrases of her favourite concerto.

Adam sat perfectly still, staring at her, throughout the first movement. Finally she said, 'What is the matter with you?'

'You're an abominable brat, you know. And I think

I've come up with the solution. Whenever you say something insulting about my work, I'm going to kiss you.'

For an instant, there was a funny, unsettled sensation in the pit of Sara's stomach. Then she shrugged and said lightly, 'Why would you want to?'

'It's an experiment in aversion therapy. Sort of like shocking a rat to make him cut out his bad habits. You don't like to be kissed, so therefore if every time you——'

A crash echoed through the house, as loud, Sara thought, as if the roof has collapsed. A fragment of a second later, a scream rang out, and then there was a rhythmic, heavy thumping that sent Sara flying down the hall to the big staircase.

Half-way up it, the last light of evening filtered through the huge stained-glass window, and in the centre of the landing directly below it lay Olivia, her eyes closed and her face a curious shade of blue.

It took an instant for Sara to realise that Olivia wasn't dead, that the colour of her skin was because of the stained glass. She was used to the brilliant jewel colours that the window produced during the day. Now, with only the last weak rays of twilight, the colours had faded to dark, murky puddles against the carpet runner, and Olivia's face lay squarely in the centre of one.

Adam was at her side. Sara sent a wide-eyed, pleading look up at him, as if begging for him to make it all right, and knelt beside Olivia.

'I'm fine, really,' Olivia said, but she didn't open her eyes, and Sara thought she was wincing against pain. 'The stairway was dark; I should have turned on a light. Careless of me.' Then, ladylike as always, she fainted.

'What are they doing to her? What's taking so long?'

Sara paced restlessly across the hallway outside the emergency room. 'They could have X-rayed every bone in her body by now.'

'That's probably exactly what they're doing.' Adam was sitting perfectly still; the only sign of his agitation was the index fingertip that wouldn't stop tapping against the vinyl arm of his chair. 'She took a nasty fall, Sara. That's a long flight of steps.'

'There was plenty of light on the stairs, you know. So what do you think really happened?'

He shrugged. 'She may have just missed her footing.'

Sara turned that possibility over in her mind. 'I hope that's all it is, but she's past eighty, Adam. You don't think she might have had a stroke, do you?'

'I didn't see any sign of it. But I'm not an expert.'

'I suppose her sight might be going.'

'She was knitting,' he reminded.

'You must have heard her say she can do that in the dark.' The implications made her shudder.

He rose and came across the room to her. 'Don't borrow trouble, Sara. Wait and see what the doctor says.'

She sighed. 'I know. But I'm just so scared, Adam.' She put her head down on his shoulder, aware only of the comforting strength of his arm around her.

'You really care what happens to her, don't you?' he said gently.

It infuriated her. She stepped away from him and looked up with a challenge in her eyes. 'Of course I care,' she snapped. 'Did you suppose I was just like Phillip, out to get my hands on Ashton Court and not giving a damn about Olivia?' She clapped a hand to her mouth. 'Oh, God, I should call Phillip.'

'Don't rush into it. I can't speak for you, but if I had

to listen to his hypocritical ravings tonight I'd probably throw him through that window.'

She giggled, unwillingly. 'I know, but he is her nephew.'

'Which would you rather have, Sara? Phillip mad at you tomorrow because you didn't call him, or Olivia upset tonight because you did?'

'Well,' she admitted, 'if you put it that way——'

The ambulance which had brought Olivia to the hospital had gone out on another call, and the emergency room had treated an upset stomach, a sunburn, and an ear infection before Olivia's doctor came to talk to them.

'Olivia is the luckiest octogenarian around,' he reported bluntly. 'A tumble down those stairs should have been good for a broken hip at least in a woman her age, but apparently all she's done is sprain her knee. I'm going to keep her overnight for observation, though, just in case.'

Sara sagged into a chair in relief.

'It's going to be a nuisance,' the doctor warned. 'You'll have to get a wheelchair, and it'll be a week or two before she's up and running around again.'

'We can manage,' she said. 'We'll need some nursing help, perhaps, but Adam and I can handle most of it, between us.' She was surprised to see that Adam was frowning. That's some kind of thanks, she thought sarcastically. He thought it was perfectly fine for Olivia to take him in for the summer, but now that she's become a nuisance . . .

'It would help if she had a elevator in that museum she calls a house,' the doctor went on. 'I told her years ago to install one, but would she take my advice? Any woman of sense would have given that place up long ago and moved into an apartment.' He glanced at his watch. 'You can see her for a minute if you like—they're moving her upstairs to a room now.'

Sara watched him leave, and said, 'I see Phillip's been talking to him. That miserable wretch has just been waiting for an excuse——'

'Don't blame Phillip. The doctor may have got the idea all by himself.' Adam sounded preoccupied.

'And what does that mean?'

'Maybe she should give up the house, Sara. What would have happened tonight if we hadn't been there?'

'But we *were* there! And she could have fallen down a flight of stairs anywhere!'

'She's not being realistic. And neither are you.'

She dug her fists into her hips and glared at him. 'Whose side are you on, anyway?'

'Nobody's. Certainly not Phillip's. But a person doesn't have to covet Ashton Court in order to see that it makes no sense for Olivia to stay there. You can't be in the house every minute for the rest of her life, you know.'

'Well, I have no intention of leaving!'

He just looked at her, with one eyebrow raised.

'What do you care, anyway?' Sara said, nastily. 'What Olivia does is certainly not your problem!'

For a long moment, she thought he was going to ignore her. Then he said quietly, 'No, it isn't. Nevertheless, I can't say I'm anxious to leave her to Phillip's loving care. Shall we go and say goodnight to her?'

On the drive home, he said thoughtfully, 'I wonder if she is hanging on to Ashton Court for Pamela——'

'As if Pamela would want it,' Sara sniffed. 'From what I've heard about her, I doubt it. Not that I blame her, really.'

'Obsessions don't have to be sensible, Sara.'

'Well, your diagnosis is wrong this time, because Olivia has given up the idea that Pamela might come home some day.'

'Oh? And just how did you decide that?'

She hesitated. She had spoken without thinking, but now that she had got herself into the subject, it was too late to back out. She held out her hand, and the aquamarine sparkled in the glow from a streetlamp. 'This ring,' she said slowly. 'It's Pamela's. On the inside of it is engraved her name and *"Sweet Sixteen"*—it must have been a birthday present. For Olivia to give it away——'

'I see,' he said. They finished the drive in silence and let themselves into the house, which was still ablaze with lights. 'I'll lock up,' he offered. 'Go on to bed.'

But she was too tired to sleep, and too many questions revolved mercilessly in her mind to allow her rest. How would they manage, with Olivia confined to a wheelchair? How long would it be before she was back to normal? And what about the question of Ashton Court? So Adam, too, thought she should give it up.

'It's hers, dammit,' Sara muttered. 'Whether it makes any sense for her to live here or not, it's her home!' She punched her pillow into a new shape, and then flung it aside and pushed the sheet back. Some exercise was what she needed, she decided. If she wore herself out enough, her mind wouldn't be able to keep her awake.

She swam a couple of determined laps in the pool and then turned over to float on her back. Could Adam be right? she wondered. Or was he, like Phillip, playing his own game, less interested in Olivia's welfare than in the benefits he might reap from the situation? All that talk of being a vagabond, of not wanting to be tied down with possessions—was it only talk?

Not Adam, she thought. He wasn't like Phillip, or like Guy, interested only in himself. She knew it, and yet she had no evidence to back up her conviction. No evidence at all.

The door of the pool house squeaked, and she froze as a shadow crossed the moonlight-streaked tiles and stopped at the edge of the pool. 'Sara?'

She started breathing again. 'I'm in the water, Adam.'

'Don't you know you should never swim alone? It's dangerous.' He sounded half angry, half relieved. He dropped his terry robe on the tiles and slid into the water, almost without a splash. 'You should always bring a buddy along.'

Will you be my buddy? She almost spoke the words aloud, before she realised what she was thinking.

It all fitted neatly into place, then, in the brief moments that it took for him to swim half the length of the pool and surface beside her, his hair as slick and shiny and wet as an otter's coat. It all made sense: the daydreams of a winter's fire at Ashton Court, with Adam beside it; the trouble she had trying to concentrate when he was in the room; the fearsomely effective fire of his kisses, the way she couldn't keep herself from wondering just what sort of lover he would be . . .

I have no intention of leaving Olivia, she had said. But the truth was, when Adam's time at Chandler College was done, and he left this little town, if he were to ask her to go with him, she would go—because she had fallen in love with him.

CHAPTER EIGHT

ADAM pushed the dripping hair out of his eyes and shook the water off his face. 'For a minute, when I saw you crossing the lawn in your white robe,' he said, 'I thought someone had neglected to tell me that Ashton Court has a ghost. Then the moonlight hit your hair and turned it to silver, and I thought perhaps you were an angel instead. What colour is your hair, anyway? It's not exactly blonde, and yet——'

She tried to keep her voice even, but there was a tremor in it as she said, 'Honey.'

He grinned. 'Yes, darling?' It was an intimate, breathy whisper, and it caught at her throat. If only he meant it, she thought. If only he, too, felt this magic.

'Honey-coloured,' she said steadily. 'And I'm no angel.'

He touched a wet lock of her hair, and then his hand slipped to her shoulder and pulled her gently toward him. 'No. But maybe that's not such a bad thing. What would an angel see in me?'

Plenty, Sara thought, if she was smart enough to overlook your flaws and concentrate on the essence of you——

His skin was cold and wet against hers for a moment, and then the hot blood seemed to rush through them both and bind them together as if they had been touched with glue. The friction of the water lapping against her skin combined with the soft stroking of his hands on her back to create a sensual explosion that threatened to rip Sara into pieces. She let her head fall back, cushioned against the water, and Adam's mouth found the delicate hollow at the base of her throat and then crept slowly upwards, until his lips met hers. The harsh taste of chlorine startled her, but she soon forgot it in the sheer joy of being in his arms, of knowing that for this space of time she had the power to make him want her. He might not feel for her the love she had found for him, but at this moment it didn't matter. Surely, she thought hazily, it couldn't be wrong to let herself enjoy being in his arms. It was for such a short time, after all . . .

His hands crept across her ribs to cup her breasts, and the nipples seemed to strain toward the warmth of his touch. She didn't know that she was trying not to breathe at all, until her starved lungs began to ache, and she gasped suddenly and choked and pushed herself away from him.

His arm went round her swiftly, like a steel support, and held her higher in the water until she was breathing easily again. 'I told you not to swim alone,' he muttered.

'I was fine when I was alone,' she gasped.

He frowned. Slowly, as if he was reluctant to release her, his hands dropped away from her body. 'I didn't mean to frighten you, Sara. I should never have got in the water, but you must admit you're a temptation at the best of times, and in that skimpy swimsuit——'

'It wasn't you,' Sara said, incurably honest. 'I—you didn't scare me.'

'I didn't? Well, I scared the very hell out of myself.' He pushed her gently away and struck out for the edge of the pool. 'I didn't mean to let this get so far out of control.'

She climbed out on to the tiles and stood there dripping and furious. 'Who said it's out of control? If you're implying that I don't have enough command of myself to keep from jumping into bed with you——'

'Do you?' he asked with interest. 'I'm not sure I do.'

'—just because you kissed me——'

'You kissed me back, Sara, my dear—or rather, you handed me a tidy little package of nitroglycerine, wrapped up to look like an ordinary kiss. And if that had gone on for another minute, we wouldn't be standing here talking about it right now.'

'Just what makes you so certain of that?' Sara planted her hands on her hips and stared defiantly up at him. 'And if you really think I've invited that kind of conduct from you, what's keeping you from doing something about it?'

He threw a towel at her. It slapped across her face and dropped to the tiles. 'Because,' he said deliberately, 'as much as I'd like to make love to you tonight, I have just enough presence of mind left to know that if I did, I couldn't look Olivia in the eye when she comes home tomorrow.'

Sara felt as if the air had been knocked out of her. She stooped slowly to pick up the towel, and absently started to dry herself off. 'You'd be ashamed, you mean,' she said quietly.

'Hell, no! It's not a matter of my morality that concerns me. But it is Olivia's house, and her generation frowns on that sort of thing.'

She said, slowly, 'But you've been saying for a week that you wanted——' She stopped, abruptly, and bit her lip. Had all that just been a game? Had he only been playing with words, tormenting her, seeing how far she would let him go?

'To go to bed with you? Yes, I have. And I still do. But——' He paused, and then said in a rush, 'As inconvenient as it is at times, I was raised to respect my elders.'

'And you think I wasn't?' Sara asked tartly, thinking of her grandmother. I should be grateful he has some scruples left, she thought, because I've certainly forgotten about mine . . .

'I can't quite see myself asking Olivia, "Oh, by the way, do you mind if I move down the hall into Sara's room so we can conduct a torrid affair?" Olivia may adore us both, but I don't think she'd be very open-minded about that.'

Her face flamed. 'You don't need to make it sound as if I was trying to seduce you?'

'And a heck of a shock it was to me, too,' he said promptly. 'After the way you've held me at arm's length all week——'

She interrupted sharply. 'I was only wondering what you were thinking, and why you seemed to have changed your mind! I certainly didn't mean to imply that I actually wanted you to——'

Adam grinned. 'Of course not,' he said smoothly. 'And if I had invited you to go inside with me a minute ago, you'd have slapped my face in indignation, I suppose.'

'Probably.' But her voice wobbled a little, and she thought, if you had wanted to make love with me tonight, Adam, I would not have refused you. I would have forgotten all about Olivia and the fact that I'm a guest in her house . . .

'Like hell,' he murmured. 'So why don't you dash along to your lonely bed, Sara, my dear, and I'll have another dip in the pool, in lieu of a cold shower?'

'You shouldn't swim alone,' she said automatically.

'Are you offering to join me?' It was silky and suggestive. 'Sara, my dear, I never said that I couldn't be persuaded to turn my back on my middle-class upbringing.'

She slowly turned away and went back to the house, her bare feet noiseless on the sofa grass. And she watched for long minutes from her darkened bedroom window until a dim shadow slipped from the pool house and back across the lawn to Ashton Court.

Make up your mind, Sara Prentiss, she ordered herself. You can't have it both ways. There was a moment there, in the water, when you didn't give a damn about tomorrow, if you could have him tonight. You can't go around kissing him like that and then play the offended virgin when he seems to think you'd like to go to bed with him.

It's no worse than what he's done, the other half of her brain reminded. He sounded a bit like an offended virgin himself tonight, with all that talk of respecting Olivia.

Nevertheless, she thought, whatever his reasons, he was right about that. Olivia would be horrified to discover that her house-guest and her companion were carrying on an intrigue under her roof. It was pure selfishness that had allowed Sara, for a moment, to put her own desires ahead of respect for Olivia's wishes. It was Olivia's house, after all, and Olivia's rules applied whether she was there or not.

Besides, Sara added to herself, it was all for the best, anyway. There could be no good result if she slept with him. It would be hard enough as it was to see him go, without adding anything more to regret.

There was a tap on her door, so soft that it was almost inaudible.

She turned toward it with eyes wide and hesitated for a long moment. The tap was not repeated. Had he changed his mind and slipped away? Or was he allowing her to pretend, tomorrow morning, that she hadn't heard his knock?

She knew she should ignore it. In a matter of weeks he would be gone. She would be buying herself nothing but heartbreak if she let this go any further. Far better to smile about it tomorrow, and pretend those stolen kisses in the pool had been bits of a dream, than to have him for this brief moment, and then to let him take her heart away with him . . .

All that, she knew. And she knew, too, even as she crossed the room to open the door, that for her there was no turning back, and no pretending that this was only a casual satisfying of a simple bodily hunger.

'The cold shower didn't work very well,' Adam said huskily. 'I can't forget about how you feel in my arms. And I began to think that what Olivia doesn't know won't hurt her.'

'Come in,' she whispered.

Tension seemed to fade from his body. He closed the door slowly and reached for her, and she shut her eyes and gave herself into his arms, into his care. He was not Guy, and in some unfathomable way she knew that Adam would not purposely hurt her. If this sharing would inevitably lead to pain, then there would also be remembered joy to help soothe the anguish.

It began as a gentle loving. He seemed to read her thoughts, for he knew how to give her pleasure in ways that she could never have put into words. He brought her to the brink of losing her reason, then drew her back into the safe security of his care, where nothing could threaten her, and began once more, relentlessly, to build her longing for him into a furious, insatiable hunger. And when she pleaded incoherently for his possession, he whispered, with a tremor in his voice, 'No, Sara. Not until you want me as much as I want you.'

So she waited until the frenzy of impatience threatened to drive her mad, and when ultimately he came to her she discovered that the stories of stars exploding and worlds moving were not the stuff of legend, after all . . .

She couldn't breathe properly for a long time after that, much less think coherently. When she went to sleep in his arms a long time later, she felt certain, deep inside herself, that no matter what was to come she would never regret this night. His loving had left no room for doubts . . .

She woke slowly, certain that she was being tormented by a sadistic insect which had lighted on her nose and crept across her cheek to explore her ear. She swatted at it and hit something large and solid instead. It was Adam's hand, she saw when her eyes popped open, guiding a lock of her own hair on that marauding path.

'If you're going to play that sort of game,' she announced sleepily, 'don't be surprised if I hold you down and tickle you.'

'Try it,' he invited softly. 'It sounds entertaining.' But despite the gentleness of his words his eyes held a sort of watchful wariness that sent an uneasy twinge down her spine.

I can't bear it, she thought, if he tells me last night should not have happened. Even though I know it would be no more than the truth.

She eyed him uncertainly, fully awake now and uneasy.

He sighed. 'Are you having regrets?'

She didn't answer. 'We'll be late for class.'

'That's nothing new—at least for you.' But the soft teasing held a hollow note. 'I know,' he said. 'We shouldn't have done that. But damn, it was fun.'

She turned away, biting her lip, wanting to hide her face in the pillow and sob.

He kissed her bare shoulder, under the waves of blonde hair, and slipped away from her. 'I'd better go rumple my bed so Annabelle won't get suspicious.'

Fun, she thought. And was that all it had meant to him—a night of enjoyment, snatched under Olivia's very nose?

Now she knew that she didn't even have to wait for him to leave Ashton Court. Right here, right now, was where the pain began.

She sat through his class and listened as he diagnosed, with surgical precision, the faults in a student's story. She wouldn't have begun to see those things herself, she thought, but once he had pointed them out even the student agreed. She found herself reconsidering her attitude about Adam's lack of interest in his class. He didn't spend hours looking for misspelt words and misplaced commas, but perhaps he was doing something far more important.

After her own class, she went back to her office, intending to call the hospital to see if Olivia could come home. As she started down the hall, she could see that the door of her office was open, and her step slowed a bit. That meant Adam was there, waiting for her, and she didn't know quite what to say to him. There hadn't been a chance to talk this morning, with Annabelle in the house, and then their class to cope with. Not that she would have known what to say. And there had been even less time to think.

But now, apparently, he was waiting for her. Would he be completely businesslike? she wondered. Surely not; Adam was never that, no matter how serious the matter was. He would have a witty remark when she walked in, and that bothered her even more. To have last night reduced to a joke would be more than she could bear.

Then she heard another voice, raised in anger. 'You've spent the last two weeks using undue influence on Olivia. What are you trying to do, Merrill? Persuade her to leave the place to you?'

Phillip, she thought with a sinking heart, and hurried down the hall. She tried to be philosophical; this confrontation was inevitable, and at least Phillip wasn't causing a scene in the hospital corridors, where Olivia would certainly hear.

She stopped in the doorway of her office, one hand braced on the jamb, astonished at the sight inside. Adam was lounging in her desk chair with his back toward the door and his feet propped on the corner of her blotter. An open bag of corn chips was in his lap, and he was munching one after another and seemingly ignoring Phillip, who had braced his hands on the opposite side of the desk and was leaning over it threateningly.

'And thanks for your helpful suggestion about standing up to Olivia and telling her what's what,' Phillip went on sarcastically. 'I went to see her a couple of days ago and told her in no uncertain terms what she should do. And do you know what her answer was? She said if I was trying to get myself invited to move into Ashton Court I could forget it, because she isn't running a boarding-house! Her own nephew, when she's taking in every loser off the streets without even a reference!'

'You know, I can't make up my mind about you, Phil,' Adam said plaintively. 'I thought you wanted Olivia to move out and give you the place. Would you really rather live there and sponge off her?'

'If anyone knows about sponging, it's you, Merrill!'

'Or perhaps you'd prefer it if she died soon and let you inherit it free and clear? That would be the easy way.'

'Adam!' Sara couldn't hold back her gasp of astonishment. He turned the chair a fraction of an inch and then wheeled it back to the original angle, as if he wanted to ignore her presence.

'Oh, is that what you're thinking?' Phillip asked. 'Trying to put the blame on me for her accident? Well, I wouldn't be a bit surprised if she was pushed down those steps! But I had nothing to do with it.'

'Meaning that I must have done it? And what would I have to gain, Phil? Besides losing my comfortable place to live, of course.'

'Throwing suspicion on me!' Phillip howled. 'So she'll write me out of the will!'

Adam shook his head. 'Oh, I'd be much more clever than that,' he mused. 'If I'd arranged it, I'd have made sure you were in the house when she fell.'

Phillip turned on Sara. 'And as for you,' he began wrathfully, 'I want an explanation of why I wasn't called last night. She's in the hospital, dying for all I know, and you didn't even bother to let me know.'

'Oh, don't get steamed, Phil,' Adam recommended. 'She'll be home today. Besides, it's Olivia's business who she wants around her, and she wanted Sara and me.'

'Oh? And I suppose you think that gives you permission to poke into her past, too, and dig up all the ancient rumours about Pamela? I've half a mind to tell Olivia myself about how you're prying into her affairs —poking around the dusty old records at the courthouse, and asking nosy questions of all the old-timers. That should get her goat; it might even get you thrown out of Ashton Court, Merrill, if I tell her the truth.'

'Phillip, don't be an idiot.' Sara threw her books down on the corner of her desk. 'It might not be the most tactful thing to enquire about, but surely you don't think anyone could be upset if Adam satisfied his curiosity?'

'Is it only curiosity? Ask him,' Phillip said, jerking his head toward Adam. 'He's dug up enough dirt to make Olivia a public laughing-stock all over again.'

'Have you found out more?' Sara asked eagerly. Momentarily, Phillip was forgotten.

He shook his head. 'Nothing much.' His eyes were still on Phillip.

'Isn't it bad enough that he's eating Olivia's food and sleeping under her roof?' Phillip said. 'What are you up to, anyway, Merrill? Trying to find out enough about Pamela so you can bring a fake in to claim the whole works?'

Adam didn't move, but his long body seemed to tense in the chair, as if he would like to spring across the desk at Phillip and choke the life from him. 'No,' he said evenly.

'Then why are you poking around the courthouse?' Phillip challenged.

'There's no law against looking up old records,' Sara put in. Both of them ignored her.

'Research.' Adam was chasing the last corn chip around the bottom of the bag, and he didn't look up. 'There's a funny thing about research,' he mused. 'You find one thing you wanted to know, and about a hundred other things that you didn't. But sometimes one of the hundred turns out to be the important one, after all.' He crunched the chip between strong teeth, and looked up at Phillip. Sara had never seen quite that look of flinty hardness in his eyes before.

'I didn't come here to listen to a lecture on what you'd like to think is a real job,' Phillip sneered. 'I want to know what you're looking for.'

'I'd rather tell you about what I accidentally found,' Adam said deliberately. 'Like the unofficial partnership between you and the contractor, Phil. And the agreement you've made to tear down Ashton Court as soon as Olivia's dead, and build apartments on the site.'

Sara gasped.

'That's completely—there's nothing like that——' Phillip sputtered.

'Nothing in writing perhaps, Phil.' Adam's voice was relentless. 'But don't bother to deny it. I have got you cold.'

'I can't imagine where you got the idea that I would have anything to do with——'

'Ashton Court is very close to the campus,' Adam said thoughtfully. 'That makes it prime development property, probably the best there is in town right now, with the college booming.'

'I had never considered such a scheme.'

'It's a big lot, too. Room for a hundred units of student housing.' Adam crumpled the empty cellophane bag and flung it at the waste-basket. 'At least, that's what the secretary in the city zoning department told me you were planning to build.'

'My God,' Sara whispered. And the tiny voice in the back of her brain reminded, of course it was a secretary who told him. I wonder how much of his charm it took to persuade her to talk . . .

She shook her head to clear it, and turned to stare at Phillip. Was he capable of such blatant scheming?

Was that what had lain behind his supposed concern for Olivia's health and happiness all along—the desire to possess not Ashton Court itself but the valuable land on which it sat? Was Adam right, or could he have made a horrible mistake?

She could see the truth of it in Phillip's eyes, in the sag of his shoulders. He had been caught, and all the bluster in the world, all the denials, all the lies, wouldn't save him now.

'It's the only thing that makes sense,' he said. His voice was low and hoarse. 'That place is from another age—all that space and all that land, that could be put to much better use.'

'Building little cracker boxes one on top of the other?' Sara whispered. 'You would destroy the beauty of Ashton Court to build one more horrible stack of apartments?'

'I'm only being practical,' Phillip said defensively. 'Who's ever going to want it, besides Olivia? Who but her would want to live in that kind of decadent grandeur? Eight bedrooms—nobody needs that kind of room these days. Nobody wants it.'

'I should have known from the first that you didn't care about the house,' Sara said crisply.

'It's not a house, it's a damned mausoleum. You said yourself it could be cut into condos.'

'Don't you even recognise sarcasm when you hear it? No, of course you wouldn't, Phillip.'

'Condos wouldn't work, you know.'

'I'm sure you've looked into it,' Sara snapped. 'Have you no appreciation of beautiful things? Ashton Court is a work of art.'

'Ashton Court is an obscenity,' Phillip said loudly, warming to his subject. 'It should never have been built; it was a vulgar and tasteless display of wealth when Otto and Olivia put it up——'

'You are certainly the authority on vulgarity and tastelessness!' Sara was almost shouting.

'Would you rather see it standing there empty and falling in once Olivia's gone?'

'It's not up to me! And it's certainly not yours to dispose of yet!' She slammed her fist down on the desk. 'Dammit, Phillip——'

'It's a waste of resources for one old woman to keep all that space and land tied up for herself, and if you were honest, you'd admit it.'

She spun around. 'Adam, tell him he's an ignorant, deluded fool, and then throw him out of my office!' she demanded.

For a moment, she didn't think he'd even heard her. He was rubbing his knuckles along his jaw, and there was a solemn set to his face as he watched the quarrel rage. 'I'd love to. But on this one, Sara, I happen to agree with him,' he said finally. 'The era is past for homes like Ashton Court—I've heard you say so yourself. And perhaps there are better uses for it, and for the land.'

Phillip grinned genially at her and turned to Adam. 'Maybe we ought to have a long talk,' he began confidingly.

'Perhaps we should,' Adam agreed. It was very smooth, and he smiled as he said it.

It seemed to Sara that everything in her field of vision had suddenly turned a nauseatingly violent shade of green. She stared across the desk at the man she had thought she loved. Horror wrenched her insides till she thought she must be screaming with the pain of it, and yet neither of the men seemed to notice. She made a hopeless little gesture with both hands and turned towards the door, knowing that she had to get away before she started to throw things at both of them.

Adam called her name when she was half-way down the hall. She hurried her step, but he broke into a run and caught her at the top of the stairs, spinning her around to face him. 'Sara, surely you don't think——' he began.

'What am I to think? Shouldn't you be in there cutting your deal with Phillip, while he's still willing to negotiate?' Her voice was bitter.

'I'm not going to make a deal with him.'

'Oh?' It was almost polite. 'You're going to insist on having it all for yourself?'

'Sara, don't sound so harsh. Surely you can't believe that I——' He paused. 'Look, I'm sorry you had to hear all that.'

'I'll just bet you are, now. But it didn't seem to bother you when I walked in. Did you think I'd take your side?'

'I could really use your help, Sara, and your support, and your trust.'

'Oh, could you?' Her voice was so bitter that her throat ached as she formed the words. 'Was that why you slept with me last night—in the fond belief that I'd be so blinded by your skill and charm in bed that I would help carry out your little scheme? All that talk about respecting Olivia, about obeying her wishes—it was all just fiction, wasn't it? Well, I won't listen to any more of it!'

'Don't be a fool, Sara.' It was sharp.

She looked up at him for a long moment, and then said, very quietly, 'Oh, no, I've finished with that, Adam.' She started down the steps.

She knew he watched her as she went down the long flight of stairs. Her hand clenched the railing;

she needed every bit of support it offered to keep herself from staggering, but she was determined not to display that sort of weakness before him. She would not give him the slightest excuse to think that she might feel regret about what she had just done. That would only encourage him to try again to persuade her to co-operate with his plans.

But it was not regret she felt, only the bone-crushing, weary weight of disillusionment.

It had all happened once again. A man she had trusted, a man she had loved, had betrayed her. But this time, she thought, it was even worse than before. Despite all his promises and assurances, Guy had never kept his marriage a secret, and she supposed that she had always known, in the buried depths of her soul, that a man who was capable of cheating on his wife shouldn't be trusted in anything else, either.

But with Adam it was different. She had grown to believe in his honesty, in his concern for Olivia. She had thought his liking for the old lady was as sincere as her own; he had certainly behaved to Olivia as a son would have, or a nephew. To find out that all of that was false, a façade built of wisps and spider webs and hiding a cold-blooded desire for profit, was a harsher blow than Sara had ever had to absorb before. It was as if not a single fragment of the man she had come to love in the past few weeks was real.

She had likened him once to a sunbeam bouncing around a mirrored room. It was impossible to catch him, impossible to know even which image was the right one. Now she knew that even the sunbeam itself had been false, an artificial light aimed to gain a purpose.

She would, of course, have to tell Olivia. It was the only honest, decent thing to do.

But what would that accomplish? she asked herself. Olivia would certainly never leave Ashton Court to Phillip, once she knew that he intended to destroy it. But what alternative was there? 'She can leave it to Adam,' Sara told herself tartly, 'so he can do the same thing!'

At least Phillip had the right of blood to the land, to the house. Poor Olivia, she thought. It will break her heart, and in the end it will all be the same, anyway.

Her head was aching from all the implications. After last night, he was so certain of me, she thought, that even when I walked into that office, into that scene, he thought I would not upset his plans.

Just the thought of how she had given herself so completely to him with love and trust and longing in her heart made her feel ill.

That afternoon, as soon as Olivia was settled into her own bedroom at Ashton Court, Sara told her, as gently as she could, and was startled because it seemed that Olivia was attempting to comfort her, and not the other way around.

'Olivia, did you know about Phillip?' she demanded finally. 'What he was planning to do to Ashton Court, I mean.'

'Not exactly,' Olivia admitted.

The vague hope which had flourished for a moment in Sara's mind—the hope that Adam might have told the old woman about his discovery—died. Of course, she reminded herself, even if he had told Olivia the truth, it might have only meant that he was manoeuvring to step into Phillip's shoes. But he hadn't; he must have decided that half a prize would be better than taking the chance of losing everything.

'But I've never had any illusions about what Phillip

is capable of,' Olivia went on. 'So it's really no surprise. And I can't say that Phillip's plans are really of much concern to me.'

Sara sat for a long moment beside Olivia's bed, waiting for her to go on, but the old lady offered no further comment. So what does that mean? Sara asked herself. Are Phillip's plans of no concern because she really doesn't care what happens to Ashton Court, once she's not here to see it? Or does she mean that she's already chosen to do something else with it?

'Olivia,' she began warily, 'you can't mean that you've decided to leave the place to Adam——'

Olivia raised her neatly pencilled eyebrows and said, with a note of soft surprise in her voice, 'Why on earth would I consider giving my property to Adam?'

Sara found herself stammering, like an embarrassed child. 'Because he's very charming, and——'

'I may be an old woman, but I hope I'm not such a foolish one as that,' Olivia said gently.

'Then you see through him?' She said it slowly and almost with regret. If even Olivia had seen what she herself had missed—that fatal flaw in Adam's character that allowed him to use people like pieces of a jigsaw puzzle with no regard for their feelings——

You're the foolish one, Sara Prentiss, she told herself. You're the one who couldn't see the truth when it was battered over your head. To think that I actually believed myself in love with him!

'I do apologise, Olivia,' she said softly. 'I've underestimated you.'

Olivia smiled. 'I think I'll nap now,' she said, and Sara kissed her cheek and obediently rose to leave. 'I wonder,' Olivia went on, 'do you think Adam would mind helping me downstairs for dinner? That's going to be the worst of it, I'm afraid, if I can't get from one floor to the other.'

Sara turned in amazement. 'You're not going to ask him to leave?'

'Why should I?' Olivia sounded startled at the idea. 'Come now, Sara, if everyone who ever tried to pull off a scheme was isolated from polite company, the world would be a pretty dull place to live.'

'I suppose that's true. But——'

'Besides, he'll come in handy,' Olivia added practically. 'My doctor is right—I should have put in an elevator years ago.'

There was some amusement to be found in that, Sara thought wryly. Obviously Olivia wasn't as innocent a soul as she appeared!

When Sara went downstairs, she found Adam pacing the parquet floor in the lower hall. 'If you're lurking down here waitig for a chance to sneak up to see Olivia,' she said firmly, 'don't bother.'

His jaw tightened, but he said, pleasantly enough, 'Does that mean you've convinced her not to see me at all?'

'I haven't that much power. You can talk to her at dinner—she wants your help to come down.' She walked past him and said, 'In case you're wondering how much of a story to create, I told her everything.'

'Do you feel better now that you've interfered? Does it give you some sort of perverted pleasure to manipulate things, Sara?'

She wheeled around to stare at him in disbelief. 'What do you mean, *I'm* manipulating things? How can you dare say such a thing to me, Adam Merrill?'

'It's Olivia's property, dammit—will you get it

through your head that it's up to her to decide, not you?'

'Isn't that the whole point? I just gave her the facts.'

'You're so eager to run to Olivia with the worst possible interpretations of everything that it begins to sound to me like you're trying to get it for yourself.'

Sara gasped. 'You know perfectly well I don't give a damn about this place! It's Olivia I care about!'

'And of course, you know what's best for her,' he mocked. 'You're even more of an expert on the subject than she is.'

She said tightly, 'I don't care to listen to you any more, Adam.'

'I know. You've already said that. Well, I'm glad you gave me this little illustration of faith and trust, Sara. If this is what it means to you, I can do without it.'

He stalked off, leaving her standing in the hall with her mouth open. As if, she thought helplessly, he expected her to refuse to believe in the evidence of her own eyes and ears.

For the next few days Ashton Court seemed like one long tea party. It was never quiet; Olivia seemed to be entertaining her entire circle of friends, a few at a time, around her wheelchair or gathered by the fainting couch in her morning-room.

For Sara, it was a long and silent few days. She stopped going to Adam's early-morning class, and spent most of her time in her room. Not even Olivia seemed to need her; when her friends went away, she summoned Adam . . .

Sara and Adam met only at the dinner-table, on the nights when he brought Olivia down. He made no move to improve conditions between them; though they talked when it was necessary, it was brittle, surface conversation, without a hint of the teasing and heckling that had marked the first few weeks. Sara told herself stoutly that it was a relief, but she couldn't quite make herself believe that she didn't miss it.

Olivia's week of recovery was almost over when Sara went into her bedroom one afternoon to find her staring out the casement window at the rose-garden and holding a letter. At first, Olivia didn't hear her, and Sara was beside the wheelchair before the woman looked up, startled.

'What are you so absorbed in?' Sara asked lightly. She couldn't keep herself from looking at the stationery in Olivia's hand—a pale ivory, with an envelope lined in a brilliant paisley paper, addressed in a firm, feminine hand.

'It's just a get-well note from Adam's mother,' Olivia said. 'So sweet of her. Read it, if you like.' She thrust the sheet of paper at Sara.

Sara fought a swift battle with herself, and yielded. It was a pleasant enough little note, she thought, just the kind of gentle, reassuring thing she would expect from a minister's wife, signed, 'Affectionately, Susan Merrill.'

'Very pleasant,' she said, dropping the letter back into Olivia's lap. 'And charming of her to send her fondest wishes to me, too.'

'Adam must have mentioned you.'

That sent chills of fear rocketing up Sara's spine. She told herself firmly that there were some things no man told his mother, and said, 'I won't count on the accuracy of it. His character portrayals are wonderful in fiction, but I'm not sure he knows what character is in real life.'

Olivia looked unhappy, but she didn't pursue it. 'Would you ask Adam if he'd help me downstairs? I'm expecting my solicitor later.'

Her solicitor, Sara thought with foreboding. She had begun to think that perhaps the whole thing hadn't mattered at all to Olivia, that her plans were already made, and nothing Phillip or Adam could do would change them. 'If you're working on your will, Olivia——'

'I'm rewriting it.'

Sara swallowed hard. 'I know this is a terribly tactless thing to say; no one's ever supposed to talk about wills——'

'Why shouldn't they?' There was only patient interest in Olivia's voice. 'Someone's got to. I thought perhaps you'd like to have the little desk that's in your sitting-room, and——'

'Olivia, I don't want anything, not a single thing. And I certainly don't want you to think that I——' She gulped. 'That I might expect to get——'

'Ashton Court,' Olivia said placidly. 'Yes, dear. I quite understand. What you're really saying is that I can't get myself off the hook about Ashton Court by leaving it to you and letting the two of them fight it out over the house and you, too.'

As if either of them would bother, Sara thought, and caught herself up short. As if I would want either of them, she told herself firmly.

'That's awfully blunt, Olivia, but—yes, that's what I mean.'

Olivia smiled and tucked Susan Merrill's letter into her portfolio, ready to be answered. 'Sorry about the bluntness,' she said gently. 'Sometimes I'm afraid I'll never grow up to be a lady. Would you get Adam, please?'

Sara hesitated. Adam was in his room, she knew, and the last thing she wanted was to confront him there.

'Or perhaps I could walk down the stairs,' Olivia said hopefully. 'My knee is really much better, and I'm so tired of this wheelchair.'

Sara tried to keep her voice steady. 'I'll get him for you.'

The irregular rattle of typewriter keys nearly stopped her. She paused for a long moment outside his room, listening, and then knocked firmly on the door.

'Come in.' It was a bad-tempered growl, and Sara would have retreated if it hadn't been Olivia's request she was passing on. She pushed the door open, and he looked up from the desk.

My God, she thought, how very good-looking he is. Those eyes—such a strange colour, and not, as she had once thought, because of contact lenses. They were really his, and she wanted to forget everything that lay between them and drown herself in the violet-blue depths. The unruly dark hair that she longed to run her fingers through, the strong body that she wanted to caress and to hold close, as she had that single night she had spent in his arms . . .

'Olivia wants you,' she said uncertainly.

'I should have known you wouldn't have come here for any other reason.' He pushed himself away from the desk and stood up. 'Sara, you've been avoiding me for days. We're going to settle this, and we're going to do it now.' He came toward her slowly.

Sara automatically retreated behind a wing-backed chair by the fireplace and spread her fingers across the top of it, as if it was a shield.

He stood and looked at her for a long moment. 'My God, you're beautiful,' he said huskily. 'I can't think about you without remembering how you looked that morning, half-awake, with my kisses still on your lips——'

'If you think that's going to change anything, Adam——'

He took hold of the chair and set it aside as if it was a bit of doll-house furniture. Before she could do more than utter a startled cry, he had seized her and pulled her against him. She tried to fight him off, and he said under his breath, 'Deny this if you can, Sara.' Then his mouth came down on hers.

She gulped and choked and tried for a moment to push him away. Then, as his lips gentled against hers, the traitorous coward inside her went weak and soft and willing in his arms. He was so very charming and, despite his shortcomings, love couldn't die so suddenly . . .

She didn't hear the soft whisper of the wheelchair in the hall. She didn't hear anything at all until Olivia said, 'What's taking so——' and then stopped, as if someone had cut her vocal cords in the middle of a word.

Sara turned to look at her, and was horrified by the stark, pasty white of Olivia's face, so unlike the healthy glow she'd had just minutes ago.

It's shock, she thought. Coming in here, after what I just said to her about Adam, and finding me in his arms. But surely that wouldn't make her ill? Unless she thinks I've been playing a part, as well—that everything I've said has been a lie——

Then she realised that it was not the two of them that Olivia was looking at, but something over their heads, something on the shelf above Adam's desk.

Olivia's blue eyes turned reproachfully to Adam, and she whispered, her voice cracked and painful and accusing, 'Where did you get Buddy?'

CHAPTER NINE

SARA'S eyes flashed up to the shelf, to the battered toy dog sitting patiently between the collegiate dictionary and the book of quotations, his head hanging over the edge as if to watch his owner at work.

'Buddy?' she whispered.

Adam had gone as white as the sheet of paper in his typewriter carriage. He released Sara and stepped away from her to stare at Olivia. Sara sat down on the end of the bed, her knees shaking too much for her to stand. She watched him in horrified fascination as he clenched and unclenched his fists, almost in slow motion. Adam, without a ready quip? she thought. Adam, without words at all?

'Where did you get Buddy?' Olivia repeated. Her voice cracked. She shifted herself in the wheelchair as if she was going to stand up.

'I've—I've always had him.' Adam's voice was lifeless, as if he didn't know what he was saying. It was the same answer, Sara thought, that he had given her, the day she had found the dog and put him up there. 'He was my mother's.'

'Susan's.' Olivia's voice was dead and dull. Then she clutched the arms of the wheelchair till her knuckles showed dull yellow, and said, 'No, by God, he can't have been. Give him to me!'

Adam seemed to be frozen to the centre of the floor. It was Sara who reached up for the limp little figure and put him gently into Olivia's lap.

The old woman touched the worn fur with a gentle

153

finger. She turned the toy upside-down to inspect the stitching, and looked carefully at the button eye. Then she blinked back tears and said, in a voice that quavered and showed every one of her eighty-two years, 'He lost that eye in a slumber-party squabble one night, when Pamela was ten——'

My God, Sara thought, she's gone completely crazy. She knelt beside the wheelchair and took one of Olivia's thin, wrinkled hands between both of hers. 'You know that's not possible, Olivia.'

'I don't understand what's happened,' Olivia said. 'But it's not only possible, that's how it has to be. Isn't it, Adam?'

He nodded slowly. 'It's the only thing I have of hers.'

'It actually belonged to Pamela?' Sara's voice was taut. 'How is the hell did you get hold of Pamela's——'

'And Pamela, Adam?' Olivia's voice was a bare whisper.

'I was born in a charity hospital in Philadelphia,' Adam said. 'My mother had been admitted a few days before, with a raging infection. It had apparently affected her heart, and she died during the delivery —they did everything they could. I'm sorry, Olivia.'

The old woman had put her head down into her clenched hands.

'She had very few possessions with her,' Adam said. 'The clothes she was wearing, a sorority pin, the dog.'

Olivia murmured the Greek name of a sorority, and Adam nodded. He looked a little stunned.

'That was all anyone knew about her, you see,' he said. 'She wouldn't talk about herself, and later—well, then there was no time for questions.'

'But you have parents,' Sara said uncertainly. 'You have a mother——'

His eyes had a distant look about them, a hazy

shadow in the violet-blue. 'Yes,' he said. 'I do. The
Merrills adopted me. He was the chaplain at the
hospital, and she was one of the nurses who took care
of—Pamela.' He knelt beside Olivia's chair, across from
Sara. 'I'm sorry it's been a shock to you,' he whispered.
'You see, I had come to believe this was just another
dead end for me—another possibility, another Pamela,
but not the right one. If I had known, I never would
have broken it to you this way, Olivia.'

'Olivia,' she repeated. She pushed a wayward lock of
hair back from his forehead with a trembling hand. 'Do
you think perhaps you could learn to say *Grandmother*,
Adam?'

It was a long and disjointed story, this fitting together of
pieces known, pieces deduced, and it took most of the
evening in the telling. Sara sat in a shadowed corner of
the little morning-room, ashamed of herself for
intruding on this very private reunion, and yet unable
to muzzle her fascinated curiosity and go away.

He had always known, Adam said, that he was a
special and chosen child, and that he had had another
mother once. 'My parents made me their own,' he said,
'and in every way that counts, Cliff and Susan Merill
are my mother and father. But the fact was that they
actually knew Pamela, for those few days, and they
never hid the truth from me. What little they knew,
they told me.'

The Merrills had not tried to wipe out the bits of
heritage Pamela had left; Buddy had been an ever-
present part of his childhood, and they had named him
Adam Chandler Merrill.

'That's the name she gave when she came to the
hospital,' he explained. 'Pamela Chandler. There was
no reason to question it. It was only after she died that

the hospital realised the other information she'd given—the address, the next of kin—were non-existent.'

'But didn't they look?' Olivia whispered.

Adam shook his head. 'Not much, I'm afraid. The hospital concluded that she wasn't from Philadelphia at all, but they didn't have the resources to investigate further. Besides, she'd never mentioned a family, so there seemed no point in looking for one, and in any case they were mostly interested in getting this troublesome infant off their hands, not in seeking out Pamela's history. And since there was no crime involved, the police weren't much interested, either.'

It was gentle enough, matter-of-fact, and Olivia nodded sadly.

'I was considered an abandoned child, and the Merrills took me in. The authorities made a minimal search for my father—it consisted of a couple of ads in the newspapers, asking him to come forward and claim me. When there was no response, I was put up for adoption.'

'I want to meet them,' Olivia whispered. 'I want to tell them thank you——'

The Merrills had never discouraged him from looking for his roots, Adam said, but they had all been realistic about his chances of success. All he had was a name on a hospital record, a sorority pin, an old stuffed toy, and Cliff and Susan Merrill's impressions of the young woman they had known for a few brief days.

'I had to look,' he said. 'As an adolescent, I began to realise that she had to have come from somewhere, and also that the fact that she was dead didn't mean my father was.'

Elementary biology, Sara told herself. But it was a bit of a shock, nevertheless. She hadn't considered that part of the story. She had thought that being orphaned almost too young to remember her parents had been the harshest blow a child could receive. But the idea of growing up without a family history at all, not knowing even the true names of one's parents . . .

She remembered what he had said about the girl he had cared for once, the one whose family could be traced four hundred years back. Those parents had rejected him not because he was the preacher's kid, she realised now, but because no one knew who he was . . .

He had begun his search for Pamela Chandler at the national headquarters of the sorority, he said. Nobody knew if the pin was really hers—it was certainly an odd thing for a homeless woman to be carrying—but the Merrills thought her Midwestern accent had been an educated one. Just getting names and addresses had been a challenge, because the sorority didn't typically give out such information.

Obviously, Sara thought, there had been a young woman or two working in the office, or he'd have been there yet . . .

There had been three Pamela Chandlers who had belonged to the sorority in the decade before Adam's birth. Tracking them down, through all their moves and changes of names, had taken him years. 'And of course each was a dead end,' he said. 'Or rather, a not-dead one. One of them lives out in California and has six kids. So I had to admit that perhaps the pin wasn't Pamela's at all, just something she'd acquired. So I switched to looking for Chandler families all over the nation.'

'Census records,' Sara murmured, despite her intentions of keeping quiet.

Adam didn't seem to object to the interruption, but he didn't look at her. 'No good. They're not released for years and years. And even though the name isn't

very common, there are one heck of a lot of Chandlers
in the United States. Eventually, I was forced to admit
that perhaps her name hadn't been Chandler after
all—if she'd made up an address, she could have made
up a name, too.'

Despite her intentions of remaining aloof, Sara could
feel the tension in his voice. It gripped her heart to think
of him, searching against all odds.

'I thought it must have a meaning for her of some
kind,' he went on, 'but that didn't necessarily make it a
useful clue—she could have picked it up from a book or
a billboard or from someone she knew. But usually
even people on the run won't give up their first names.
I was fairly sure she was Pamela—just Pamela—and a
lot of good that was doing me! But I just couldn't quit
looking, either, even after there were no clues left, and
no good leads . . .'

'I know,' Olivia said. She put out a hand to him.

'Several times I made up my mind to stop beating my
head against locked doors. I told myself it was a waste
of time—all I had, after all, besides a first name, was an
old stuffed dog that could have come from anywhere.
For all I knew, she might have picked it up from a
garbage can that day on her way to the hospital.' He
glanced at Buddy, on the table beside his chair.

'He was Pamela's favourite possession,' Olivia
mused.

'Did you know she had taken him?' Sara asked.

'Yes,' Olivia said. 'At least, we knew he was gone.
But it still didn't mean she'd left on purpose, you see.
She still slept with him. That sounds a bit odd, perhaps,
but you know how girls are sometimes—they get
attached to the strangest things, and they don't care
what anyone else thinks.' She picked up the toy and
stroked his battered fur. 'I suppose it was partly

because he was from the days when we were just an ordinary family—before Otto's patents and inventions became successful, and we started to build Ashton Court. I think that was when we began to lose Pamela.' There was no bitterness or guilt in her voice, just sadness. She looked up at Adam with a wavery smile. 'Oh, I'm so glad you didn't give up!'

'I did on several occasions, for months at a time. I told myself that I could waste the rest of my life searching, or I could decide that who my mother was and where she came from didn't matter, and go on from there.'

Sara thought, that's almost exactly what I told him. *It doesn't matter what some ancestor did, but what you are* . . .

'And then last spring,' he said slowly, 'Dave Talbot came up to me after I'd given the commencement address at our university and said, "I wonder if you'd like to come out to Chandler College and give our students the benefit of what you've said here today." And before I knew what I was saying I'd told him that my summer was free, and I would be glad to come.'

'Chandler College,' Sara said doubtfully. 'Just that, and you came running out here?'

'That was all.' He looked at her for the first time, and his eyes were hard. 'And if you're thinking it sounds pretty silly to drop everything and rush off on a wild-goose chase like that—well, believe me, Sara, I've done sillier things.'

The harsh tone of his voice made her shudder. 'I'm sorry,' she whispered. 'I didn't think——' Everyone could see the pain this had caused for Olivia, she thought. Pamela, she thought, had been a spoiled, self-centred brat to the end. But what about the scars it had left on Adam?

'As a matter of fact,' he went on, 'the first day I was here I nearly packed up and left, because it was such a damn-fool thing to do——'

And because of me, she thought, and the fight over how that class was to operate. 'I have to admit I was awfully surprised when you stayed,' she murmured.

He smiled at her for the first time in days, and she felt as if a warm cloud of air had surrounded her. Then she realised that the smile really wasn't for her, but for Olivia. 'That was when you started to tell me about Ashton Court,' he reminded the old woman, 'and what a joy it had been to raise your daughter Pamela there.'

Sara said softly, 'And the next day I cheerfully told you the details. And then you knew——'

'Oh, no. All I knew was that now I had two mysterious Pamelas—I was a long way from proving they were the same person. For one thing, the dates didn't work out, and when I located the precise year of the disappearance, it just got worse, because this Pamela was a lot younger than my parents judged my mother to be. The discrepancy could be explained away, but it was only speculation—I couldn't prove a single thing. And then there were little things—Sara told me that Pamela disappeared from her dormitory room, not a sorority house. And she didn't sound like a sorority type.'

'She was only in her first year at Chandler,' Olivia said. 'Back then, the college's rules said freshman had to live in the dormitories.'

'She couldn't live at home instead?' Sara asked.

A sad smile touched Olivia's face. 'She couldn't wait to leave Ashton Court.'

'I'm sorry,' Sara said. 'But in all that digging you did, Adam, there must have been something——'

He shook his head. 'I can tell you lots of things that I didn't find. I didn't turn up any hint that Pamela Reynolds might have been pregnant when she disappeared.'

'Was that why she went?' Olivia sounded very sad.

'Considering the dates——' Adam shrugged. 'It's possible. I was born seven months later, but I was premature. The fact is, however, that I couldn't find any man in her life at all. So, you see, everything seemed to say that it was just a coincidence, and not the right Pamela after all. Even Buddy was no help. Sara put him up on that shelf the day I moved in, but after that everyone politely ignred the fact that I'm a thirty-three-year-old man who carried a stuffed dog around with me. Annabelle dusted that room every day, and Buddy obviously meant nothing to her.'

'She came to work for me years ago, that's true,' Olivia said. 'But it was after Pamela——' her voice broke, and then she said firmly '—ran away.'

At least she knows, Sara thought. Any truth can be borne; it's not knowing that drives people to the brink of insanity.

The doorbell chimed and she jumped up from her chair. Olivia's solicitor was on the doorstep, a briefcase under his arm, his hat in his hand. She showed him into the library and went to tell Olivia. Adam wheeled the old lady's chair down the hall.

Sara curled herself into the window-seat, her legs pulled up and her arms crossed on top of her knees. What a heart-rending story, she thought. What a heck of a book this would make—it would be spellbinding, best-selling fiction. She had felt the same roller-coaster lift and plunge of emotions when she'd read that last book of Adam's.

Fiction, she thought. And we fell for it, Olivia and I. Every word, every nuance, every detail.

No, she told herself, remembering the white shock on Olivia's face when she saw the little dog. It all fitted together too well to have been made up. Even if Adam had found that toy somewhere in Ashton Court's attic, he could not have predicted the effect it would have on Olivia. And Olivia knew that Pamela had taken the dog with her, on that final journey . . .

It had to be true. He had the luck of the very devil himself, she thought, forgetting the moment a little earlier when she had empathised with the pain he had suffered.

'Looking for a resemblance?' he asked, from the doorway. There was a note in his voice that was almost a challenge.

Only then did she realise that she was staring at the portrait of Otto above the fireplace. She remembered seeing Adam studying it more than once, and the matching portrait of Olivia in the library, with more than casual interest. She had thought he was abstracted, absorbed in his own thoughts, scarcely seeing his surroundings at all.

'And not finding much,' Sara agreed.

His eyes blazed. 'I suppose you've concluded that I faked the whole thing.'

'I don't quite see how you could have.' It was quiet. His eyes seemed to soften, and he came quickly across to her. She uncurled from her perch in the window-seat and looked up at him, and said very deliberately, 'But then, you've had far more practice than I have in plots and schemes, Adam. Right down to your deal with Phillip.'

He swore under his breath and paced the room once, quickly, then came to a halt in front of her. 'Dammit, Sara——'

'Did you tell Olivia's solicitor how excellent his timing is, from your point of view? Just think, Adam, by midnight you could be the heir apparent.'

'Will you stop it, Sara?'

The anger in his eyes sent a shiver of remorse through her, but her disastrous tongue kept right on. 'In case you're thinking of trying your own peculiar brand of persuasion once more, as you did up in your room this afternoon, don't. Because I didn't have a chance to slapo you then doesn't mean I wouldn't do it now.'

'I have no desire to kiss you again, that's for sure.' His voice was hard.

It hurt. Making love to her must have also been just the expediency of the moment, she thought. She didn't question that he had enjoyed that night in her bed, but there had obviously been other things on his mind as well . . . Too many other things.

She struck back. 'And you also have no need to keep me on your side now, is that it? What a shame that you made that deal with Phillip today. You could have had it all. Or do you intend to back out of your arrangement? Perhaps I should warn him to look out for himself—I've heard the honour code among thieves is a bit thin sometimes.'

He turned on his heel and stalked out of the room. Sara bit her tongue till it ached. She wanted to run after him and apologise for those rash, hurtful words, but she knew that their sting could never be taken away.

And in any case, she told herself, there was nothing between them that was worth an attempt to salvage, anyway.

Olivia looked fifteen years younger the next afternoon when Sara came in to find her having coffee with Dave Talbot in the drawing-room. 'Do join us,' Olivia said.

'Isn't this the damnedest thing—the business about Adam, I mean?' Dave chimed in. 'It's the most incredible——'

If I have to listen to one more person singing his praises, Sara thought, I'm going to break one of Olivia's precious Haviland saucers and slit my wrists with the pieces. 'No, thank you,' she said politely. 'I'll leave you to enjoy your coffee. But I'd like to talk to you later if I may, Olivia.'

The old lady looked at her for a long moment. 'Of course, dear.'

Sara went up to her room and closed the door. Adam's room has been silent when she passed, his door open. Doubtless he was out celebrating, she thought, or talking to Phillip's contractor friend, or just walking the perimeter of his new-found kingdom . . .

'I wonder what Dave Talbot will think the day the wrecking ball hits Ashton Court's front entrance,' she muttered. 'Will he still think Adam is wonderful then?' The sound of the words, the harsh image they brought to mind, makde her feel ill. All the solid grand beauty that was Ashton Court, lying in a heap of broken brick and rubble? How could anyone dream of doing such a thing to all this grandeur? And how could Olivia close her eyes to it?

The answer was simple enough. 'Because he's Pamela's son, and she can't deny him anything,' she told herself.

Or had he perhaps changed his mind,? she wondered. Now that Ashton Court had a family meaning, perhaps he would preserve it. With Olivia's money backing him, he would have no need to profit from an apartment complex. Perhaps he would settle in and make it a writer's fairy-tale retreat.

She couldn't quite bring herself to believe it. The self-described vagabond, settling down? He might tell Olivia he would, she thought, but Sara could not bring herself to believe that he might actually mean it.

And that was why she had to talk to Olivia herself,

and soon.

Half an hour later the old lady knocked on the door of Sara's suite. 'You're climbing stairs now?' Sara asked, when she opened it.

'Oh, my dear, I feel so much better today. You can't imagine what it's done for me——'

'Yes, I know,' Sara said hastily. She led Olivia into the small sitting-room and gestured to a chair, then seated herself cautiously on the very edge of the matching one.

'I think I'll have a party next weekend,' Olivia said. 'A very large, very elaborate party—the kind Ashton Court hasn't seen in years.'

The kind that stopped when Pamela left, Sara thought. 'Do you think you should? All the strain, and everything there is to do—your knee can't be completely healed by then, you know.'

Olivia waved away her concern. 'I may be injured and house-bound for a few weeks, Sara, but I'm certainly not dead.'

'I didn't mean to imply——'

'I'll hire some help for Annabelle, and we'll have the caterers and the florist do the real work. If you insist, I'll sit in my wheelchair like a good girl and direct everything—will that please you?'

'But surely there's no rush,' Sara said desperately. 'You can have a party any time.'

'It's fine to delay the telling of bad news, but good news should be celebrated as soon as possible. Now, what did you want to talk to me about, Sara dear?'

Sara gave up. There was no dealing with Olivia when she was in this frame of mind. She wondered if Adam would find the knack of it; Pamela never had, and Sara herself wasn't doing much better. But then, she told herself, I'm not going to need to try much longer. It's

Adam's problem now, to take care of Olivia.

She took a deep breath. 'Olivia, I'm sure you'll agree that it's time I moved out of Ashton Court.'

Sara had braced herself for a fuss, and she had marshalled all her arguments. She had even planned, if Olivia argued, to say that perhaps it was time to move on, and she was thinking of looking for a position with another college as soon as she could.

But, instead of arguing or exclaiming or fussing, Olivia merely smiled and said, in a soft murmur, 'Well, yes, I suppose it is, dear. But surely you don't mean to leave before I'm back on my feet, Sara? And the party—you'll have to stay for that, of course.'

As if she doesn't give a darn what I do, Sara thought. As if she's eager to have me go. It doesn't matter a millimetre whether I'm here or not!

She swallowed hard and thought, of course it doesn't matter. She's got her precious grandson now, and that's all she cares about. They're a selfish pair who deserve each other, and I wish them both joy.

She choked back a sob. After all, the two years that she had lived at Ashton Court had been a very special time. I thought we were friends, Olivia, she wanted to say. Really friends.

But she didn't say it. She was afraid that Olivia would think she wanted to stay on, after all, and that the old lady would feel sorry for her.

Sara reached out for a small velvet box on the table and put it into Olivia's hands, quickly, before she could change her mind.

Olivia opened it and looked for a long moment at the aquamarine ring, sparkling against the white velvet lining of the case. 'What on earth——' she began.

'It was Pamela's, wasn't it? I can't be mistaken.'

'Yes, but——'

'Then it should be Adam's now.'

Olivia turned the ring box and then looked up with a gleam of humour in her eyes. 'I can't see him wearing it, you know.'

'That's not the point. He's got sisters—some day he'll have a wife, no doubt, and perhaps a daughter.' It hurt to say the words. 'It belongs to him.'

Olivia raised a neatly plucked eyebrow the fraction of an inch. 'But, Sara, I couldn't possibly take it back. I gave it to you, before I had any idea——'

'I didn't ever consider it a gift, just a loan. I knew it was far too valuable to accept, even before I knew who it had belonged to.' She added gently, 'You had given her up, even then, hadn't you?'

Olivia sighed. 'I suppose I had. That doesn't change things, Sara. If anything, I feel even more strongly that you should have the ring. I'm sure Adam will agree.'

'Please, Olivia, don't make me give it to him myself.' It was a bare whisper, and it broke in the middle.

The old lady read the pain in her eyes. She looked unhappy, and confused. 'I don't understand,' she said. 'Yesterday——'

Sara forced herself to laugh. 'Oh, that scene you walked into in Adam's room? It was—research, that's all. I think he was plotting out a love scene for his next book, and I just happened to be handy . . .'

The old lady wrinkled her nose as if she thought the explanation smelled of long-dead skunk. Sara didn't blame her, but on short notice it was the best she was capable of. And it was better than the truth. Anything, she thought, would be better than the truth.

'Very well,' Olivia said slowly. 'If you insist on returning this, I'll give it to Adam. But I'd like to buy you another ring to take its place, Sara. Would you like an aquamarine again, or something else? A sapphire, perhaps, or a ruby?'

A ring to look at one dark winter evenings, to remind her of this summer, with all its possibilities, its promise, its passion and its pain? No, thanks, Olivia, she thought; I couldn't bear it.

Sara hadn't slept well all week, and that night was no exception. She lay awake and studied the darkness till her eyes ached, thinking that she had never before known there were so many shades of black. Finally she decided that a snack might help. It certainly couldn't hurt; she hadn't been eating much, either.

She stood at the doorway of her room and listened to the silence of Ashton Court for a long moment before she dared to pad softly along the hall and down the back stairs to the kitchen.

She was making hot chocolate when the hair began to prickle on the back of her neck, and she knew she was not alone. She didn't bother to turn around; Olivia would have spoken by now, and that left only one person who could be standing in the doorway behind her, watching.

Perhaps if I ignore him he will go away, she thought, and concentrated on stirring her hot chocolate until she felt sure her spoon had worn a groove in the bottom of the pan.

There was nothing to say, she thought. The last words between them had been the hurtful ones she had flung at him last night. They hadn't exchanged so much as a good morning today in class; he had looked straight through her. And when she had gone back to her office he hadn't been there, waiting for her. The room had felt like a tomb without his teasing presence.

He didn't leave. She waited until her nerves were taut and she could stand no more. She kept her hand steady with an effort as she poured the hot chocolate into a mug and put the pan into the sink to soak. Then she turned to face him. He was leaning against the door, his arms folded across his chest. He was barefoot, and his hair was disordered as if he'd been asleep, but he was wearing tennis shorts and a pullover.

And he looks wonderful, she thought, with a painful little sigh. She steeled herself against the sheer male attractiveness of him, and her tone was sharp as she said, 'Now that you have a personal interest in the place, are you keeping a kitchen inventory, Adam? I used a cup of milk——'

'Dammit, Sara, would you stop putting your claws out every time I come near? I haven't done anything to hurt you!'

It set her back on her heels for an instant.

'I thought you were beginning to trust me,' he said quietly. 'When you told me about Guy—and the night you let me make love to you. What happened to that?'

Trust, she thought bitterly. Yes, she had begun to trust him once, and he had taken that trust and demolished it. He had broken it as if was nothing more valuable than a plastic toy . . .

She had told him the most intimate details of her life that night, when she had shared the heartbreak Guy had caused her, but Adam had kept his own secrets safe. He had told her about the girl in his life, but he had never breathed a hint of the obsession that had compelled him to search across the miles, across the years, for Pamela. That was the driving force that had shaped him, the thing that had made him what he was. If he had truly cared for her, and trusted her, he would have told her about this most important part of his life. But he had not.

'You dare to talk to me about trust!' she said bitterly,

and turned away. 'Just go away, will you, Adam?'

There was a long, dry silence. Finally he said, 'All right, I'll leave you alone.' His voice was as flat and emotionless as if he was reciting a lesson. 'But first—Olivia gave me your ring tonight, Sara. I want you to take it back.'

She shook her head. 'It's not my ring. It never was.'

'She told me what you'd said, about it belonging to me now. Do you actually believe I would have asked for it back?'

'You would have every right to.'

'But I wouldn't do it.' He paused, and the silence stretched out before he said, so softly that she had to strain to hear, 'You see, Sara, I know why she gave it to you. Olivia herself may not really understand, but I do. It's because you've been a better daughter to her than Pamela could ever have been.'

The gentle, husky whisper sent regret and longing shuddering through every cell of her body, to the bone. Her fingers clenched on the handle of the mug. She could not look at him. She was fighting for control, afraid that if he said one more soft word she would break and run to him.

That was what she wanted to do, she realised with painful honesty, the only thing she longed for.

Perhaps he had his reasons for not telling me about Pamela, she thought. And after all, who am I to judge? I've been hurt, too . . .

She stood there clutching her mug in hands that did not feel the burning heat of the earthenware, and thought desperately, if he would only touch my cheek, and once more whisper 'Sara, my dear, the rest of the world would not matter.'

But he didn't. Instead, he said, 'Thank you for caring for and about Olivia. She's going to miss you, of course, and we can never repay what we owe you.'

The momentary gentleness was gone, and the formal tone of his voice dissolved the last fragment of hope she had clasped tightly to her. 'Please don't talk to me about debts,' she whispered. 'Olivia is—was my friend.'

She couldn't see his eyes, but she could hear the hard note in his voice. 'Please take the ring, Sara; it's a tiny thing.'

She shook her head. She didn't look at him, but she knew a moment later when he turned and silently left the kitchen.

She released the breath she didn't know she'd been holding. Then she carried her hot chocolate upstairs and let it grow cold on the bedside-table while she cried harsh and silent tears: tears of regret, of fear, of shattered dreams.

She faced the truth then, and admitted that even if she ran away from Ashton Court, away from him, she couldn't escape this pain. Her fate was to love him, no matter what he was or what he did, and the mystery of him—the conflicting forces that made him an enigma—was part of what she loved. There were hidden pieces of him that no one would ever quite puzzle out, and those fragments could entertain a woman, fascinate her, for all her life.

That was what she still wanted, Sara admitted in the all-knowing darkness: nothing more nor less than a chance to solve the riddle that was Adam Merrill.

But that challenge and that opportunity had passed forever out of her reach.

CHAPTER TEN

ASHTON COURT lay at peace under the heat of the mid-afternoon sun, but to Sara's eyes it seemed to be holding its breath in anticipation of the party to be held that night.

Don't be silly, she scolded herself as she walked up the driveway. It's only a party. And the house couldn't possibly have any feelings about it, even if it is something of a welcome for the prodigal son . . .

A car was parked by the front door. It was Phillip's, she realised, with a bit of trepidation. Had he heard the rumours, and come to confront Olivia?

As she reached the entrance, the front door was flung open and Phillip stormed out. He would have slammed the door, she thought, but the heavy, carved walnut panel would not permit such an ill-bred action. His eyes fell on Sara and he said through clenched teeth, 'That woman ought to be in an institution!' His face was almost purple, and he was sputtering. 'She actually had the gall to thank me for my interest in her affairs!'

'She's told you, then.' That was some relief; Sara had been wondering for the last couple of days if Olivia was blithely planning to surprise Phillip, along with the rest of the town, at her party when she introduced Adam as her grandson. But now it was apparent that Phillip knew. And, just as obviously, he no longer thought that Ashton Court would some day be his.

'If you can believe it,' he stormed, 'she invited me up here today to tell me about the house and ended by saying she knew I'd be delighted to welcome my new

cousin at this damned party tonight. As if I'd ever set
foot in this creepy place again!'

Good, Sara thought. At least we won't have public
bloodshed tonight.

'She actually sounded as if she was proud of herself,
if you can believe it.' Phillip sounded amazed at the
idea.

'Well, she's very happy to have found him,' Sara put
in cautiously.

Phillip glared at her, as if he hadn't quite seen her
before. 'This is all your fault, you know!'

She was astounded. 'What do you mean, it's my
fault?'

'Don't pretend innocence. You must have told her!'

'About your plans for Ashton Court? Yes, I did, as a
matter of fact. But I had nothing to do with her
decision.'

'I should sue you. And as for that damned fraud
you're helping—well, take my advice and don't count
on his splitting the proceeds with you when it's all said
and done!'

'He's not a fraud.' She was surprised herself at what
she had said; she certainly hadn't intended to stand up
for Adam.

'Are you certain of that?' Phillip asked nastily.

'That's really not the point. Can you prove
otherwise?'

'He's been manipulating her for weeks. I should sue
him, too.'

'Save your money, Phillip,' she recommended
crisply. 'It's a hopeless battle.' She had been prepared
to feel sympathy for him; he was, after all, losing a
considerable inheritance, and no one could be expected
to react to such an event with joy. But to act this way
about it, like a whiny child whose balloon had been

taken away . . . Well, Phillip was predictable, if nothing else, she thought.

'I suppose you think she's doing the fair and proper thing!'

'I think that I've got nothing to say about it, and neither do you.' Sara pulled open the heavy front door and then turned back, unable to resist a final barb. 'I seem to remember warning you a few weeks back that Olivia might have some relatives somewhere,' she reminded.

'That's right,' Phillip said, and shook a finger at her. 'And that's exactly why I think you've been in collusion with him all along!'

She shut the door in his face. Perhaps, she thought, seeking out another job wouldn't be such a bad idea, after all. There were certain things about this town, she reflected, that she wouldn't miss at all.

Inside Ashton Court there was a subdued bustle as the caterers' men set up a portable bar and began to arrange the buffet tables. The floral centrepieces had been delivered earlier in the day, and in the dining-room Olivia was painstakingly rearranging one of them.

'I thought you paid the florist to do that,' Sara said.

Olivia looked up with a smile. 'He's got good stock, but no originality,' she confided. 'Everything he does always looks the same.'

'Aren't you afraid of hurting his feelings?'

'Oh, no. He's not coming to the party tonight, so he'll never know, when people compliment him on his work, that it wasn't his, after all.' She replaced the last blossom in the china vase, reached for her cane, and started for the kitchen. 'Did you see Phillip?'

'I couldn't miss him,' Sara said drily. 'If I was Adam, I'd hire a food taster and a bodyguard.'

'Oh, it won't come to that,' Olivia said airily. 'Phillip's too much of a coward to do anything but bluster.'

It didn't seem to be bothering Olivia much, Sara thought. Well, doubtless Adam could take care of himself. If certainly wasn't Sara's problem.

'And I can't blame Phillip, of course,' Olivia went on. 'I did shatter a long-held dream of his. The poor boy was quite shocked, though I honestly can't see why he should be.'

'Please, Olivia, spare me the details.' It was sharper than Sara had intended, and she bit her lip when she saw the injured look in Olivia's eyes.

The turn-out for Olivia's party was extraordinary, and the sheer numbers made even Ashton Court's huge rooms look crowded. In fact, Sara thought as she sipped champagne in the drawing-room, it appeared as if Phillip was the only person in town who hadn't accepted the invitation. Across the room from her, Adam was surrounded by an excited group. Olivia was nearby; she was chatting with Dave Talbot, but her gaze kept slipping to Adam. And no wonder, Sara thought. He looked particularly wonderful tonight, tall and lean in dinner-clothes that fitted like a dream. He looked every inch the master of the house, and he was obviously happy with his role. He'd even got his hair trimmed. Sara wondered if that had been at Olivia's suggestion, and then scolded herself for even thinking about it. It was certainly none of her affair if Olivia started to manage his life . . .

'Incredible, isn't it?' Cynthia Talbot murmured. 'Olivia, I mean. She's trimmed another ten years off her age. I didn't think it was possible for her to look any younger.' She glanced at Sara and added, 'I'm surprised you're not over there with them.'

Sara did her best to look puzzled. 'Why should I be?' she asked gently, and went on before Cynthia could do more than look bemused, 'You look wonderful yourself tonight.' There was a suppressed excitement about the woman, she thought, not unlike the glow Olivia had been displaying all week.

I wonder what that's all about? Sara thought. I'm darned sure that it's not the same reason Olivia is going around giving off enough light to read by!

'Oh, my daughter finally got well, and she took her children home today. I love my grandchildren, Sara, but after four weeks of their constant company, I'm a wreck.' Cynthia shook her head. 'I knew I should have kept Adam. He's a lot more restful.'

That was one of the last words I would have chosen to describe him, Sara thought idly. Adam was the kind who couldn't be content with ordinary, peaceful living; if things settled down to normal, he'd go out and create a little confusion, just to keep life interesting . . . Just keeping up with the man would be a life-long challenge. Not that she would have a chance to try, she reminded herself firmly.

'But at least I'll have some time to get organised first,' Cynthia said. 'If you have any spare hours this autumn, Sara, I could certainly use an extra pair of hands.' It was a hopeful murmur.

'I may not be here.' It was almost as much of a surprise to Sara herself as it obviously was to Cynthia.

'What do you mean?' the woman asked.

Too late, Sara thought. She shrugged. 'I've been thinking that perhaps it's time to move on.'

Cynthia Talbot's eyes narrowed. 'It's funny that Dave didn't mention that to me,' she said. 'Not that he tells me every bit of the college's business, but still, I'd have thought——'

'Acually, I haven't talked to him yet,' Sara admitted.

'Of course,' Cynthia murmured. 'I see. Foolish of me.'

Sara wondered fretfully what the woman thought she saw but, before she could make up her mind to ask, Dave Talbot had climbed on to a chair and was calling for quiet. It took a while to silence the crowd. Sara swapped her empty champagne-glass for a full one as a waiter passed and settled herself against the edge of the fireplace to wait. The marble was chilly, even in the height of summer, and the cold oozed through the gauzy fabric of her dress. Adam had slipped away from the crowd that had surrounded him, she noticed, and was beside Olivia, holding her hand. The old lady looked worried, but as Sara watched he pressed her fingers and smiled down at her, and her frown eased.

How disgustingly charming, Sara thought, and wished that she'd picked up two glasses.

'Olivia has asked me to thank you all for coming tonight,' Dave began, 'to share her joy. Personally, I thought she should have decorated the place with blue balloons, stamped with "It's A Boy!" but I was overruled.'

The crowd laughed sympathetically.

'The party tonight isn't just to honour Adam, however,' Dave went on more soberly, 'but to announce a very important day for Olivia, and for Chandler College. As you all know, we're suffering growing pains over on the campus——'

He can say that again, Sara thought.

'—and Olivia, as a long-time booster of Chandler, has been aware of the need we have for more space, the kind of facility that we just can't afford to build right now. It's been a great concern to Olivia, I know, as it has to me, but because our budget is committed to providing classrooms and offices and living space for students first, our dream of a campus cultural centre has been put off time and time again. Now, as a result of Olivia's great generosity, I am pleased to announce that, by Christmas, Chandler's dream will become reality. Our cultural centre will be in operation.'

Sara's champagne-glass tipped in unsteady fingers. That's not possible, she thought. You can't draw plans and break ground for a new building like that in six months, much less have it functioning, no matter how much money you've got to spend. And surely Olivia wouldn't be making donations of that sort just now. Unless she's been planning this for a good long while, and keeping it under wraps.

When she started to think about it, she realised that Olivia had been spending a great deal of time lately with Dave Talbot . . .

'And not only a cultural centre,' he went on, above the surprised murmurs of the crowd, 'but a living museum unlike any other in the state. The lower floor of Ashton Court will become a place to hold recitals and meetings and to entertain the college's guests, and——'

Ashton Court? Sara thought. She's giving away Ashton Court?

'The upper floor,' Dave went on, 'according to Olivia's wish, will be remodelled into an apartment for the president of the college, for which my wife is most humbly grateful——'

'I can entertain in comfort again,' Cynthia Talbot said with a contented sigh. 'There is more room on that top floor than in two ordinary houses.'

Sara choked. 'But what is Olivia going to do?'

Cynthia blinked in astonishment, but she was too tactful to question why Sara didn't know. 'She's buying an apartment in the new complex they're building on the west side of town.'

The complex Phillip had suggested, Sara thought. *She thanked me for taking an interest in her affairs,* he had said that afternoon. No wonder he had been so furious; he must have taken Olivia's decision to move as a personal insult! *She called me up here to tell me about the house . . .*

She tried to tell me, too, Sara thought. And I wouldn't listen.

She looked across the room to where Olivia was almost hidden in a sea of congratulatory faces. Adam, inches taller than most of the rest of the crowd, was standing next to her.

'Thank heaven for Adam, that's all I have to say,' Cynthia Talbot said. 'It came as a complete surprise to Dave, I know, when Olivia approached him about it. How Adam was able to convince her that she should enjoy a simpler way of life for a while is beyond me, but I consider it a miracle for the college.'

Sara wasn't really listening. Cynthia's voice was a minor theme in the noise of the crowd. But the look in Adam's eyes, as she met his gaze across the room, was a very different matter; it was like a set of cymbals crashing, over and over, inside her head. She'd been right about one thing, she thought; he had been playing a deep game, a far deeper one than she had ever suspected. He had indeed plotted to win Ashton Court away from Phillip. He had schemed and manipulated and pulled every string that came into his hand. And if she had only listened, truly listened, to what he had said——

I should have known he couldn't be interested only in his own welfare, Sara thought. He isn't capable of such selfishness. If he was, he couldn't be the kind of lover he is—more interested in his partner's joy than in his own . . .

She would never know that precious sharing again. That, too, she had destroyed with her own lack of trust.

I should have known, she thought helplessly. If I had only put my faith in him, perhaps he could have shared these things with me.

Adam's eyes held hers for a long moment, with some expression in the violet-blue depths that she could not quite read. It wasn't a challenge, exactly, and yet——

But, before she could identify it, he turned away and shook Dave Talbot's hand, and grinned at him as if now he didn't have a care in the world.

At last the final person left, and the party was over. Olivia collapsed into a chair, kicked off her shoes and said, 'I had forgotten what a torment it is to entertain a crowd that size.'

Sara refrained from reminding her that the last time she had done it had been thirty-five years ago.

'It will be a relief, in a way, to have a smaller place,' Olivia mused.

'I'm happy for you, Olivia. At least I think I will be, when I get used to the surprise. I never dreamed that you would give away Ashton Court!'

Olivia looked stunned. 'But you said you were going to move, Sara! I thought you knew—I was sure Adam had told you——'

'He didn't,' Sara said gently. 'And I didn't give you a chance, did I?' She patted Olivia's hand. 'It's all right, truly it is. I understand—it's just that it was a shock.'

Olivia smiled. 'But don't you know why I've kept it all these years?' Her voice had a tiny catch. 'I wanted to be here, waiting . . .'

Sara swallowed the lump in her throat. 'And now that you know Pamela's not coming home—I see.'

Olivia nodded. But the moment of softness soon passed, and she said briskly, 'Besides, I'm not giving it up, not really. You can be certain I'll have a say in how things are run. I've got a permanent seat on the committee, and after I'm gone Adam will take my place.'

'Is he staying here, then?' Sara hoped it sounded casual.

'You'd better ask him. He hasn't told me what he intends to do. I don't think he's made up his mind.'

Sara smothered a tiny sigh.

'You needn't be in any hurry to move, Sara. My apartment won't be ready till autumn, and it will be winter before they can possibly start on the renovation upstairs. Until then, I'm sure they'd like to have someone as caretaker——'

Live at Ashton Court, alone with the memories? Sara shuddered, and tried to turn it into a shiver instead. 'It's getting chilly in here, now that the crowd's gone, isn't it? I don't think I'd be very comfortable here without you, Olivia.' She closed two of the casement windows and paused beside the big French breakfront that was the focal point of the room. 'What are you going to do with all the furniture?'

'Leave it,' Olivia said with a shrug, 'unless there's something you or Adam want.'

The linking of their names was casual, matter-of-fact, and also completely meaningless, Sara realised, when her heart settled back into its proper place. *You or Adam*, Olivia had said; not *you and Adam*. It could have been that way, she thought, if only . . . But it was fruitless to think of things like that. He had vanished the instant the party was over. It must be her that he was avoiding, she thought; it certainly wasn't Olivia.

'It's all too big for my new apartment,' Olivia said. 'I

have a fancy to start over, anyway. What do you think of a living-room carpeted in gun-metal grey, with plate-glass tables and the chairs upholstered in canvas?'

Sara looked at her in astonishment, but the old lady's china-blue eyes were serious. 'I think,' Sara said carefully, 'that you'd look like an orchid in the middle of a bowl of dandelions, Olivia.'

'Perhaps you're right. That might be a little too modern.' Olivia yawned. 'I'll have to think about it.'

Sara sat there alone in the silence for a long while after Olivia went upstairs, then she went out on the terrace. Despite the chill of the air against her bare arms and throat, there was a feeling of freedom about being outside. She sat on the terrace wall for a long time. She wasn't thinking or planning, just letting herself drift in the world of might-have-been.

She was going to have to swallow her pride, that was certain, and tell Adam that she was sorry she had misjudged him. That wouldn't make everything all right, she knew—nothing could ever do that now. Even if, once, he had been starting to care about her, she had ruined that, destroyed it with her own sharp tongue, and her own lack of faith. How could any man forgive that?

If, indeed, she reminded herself with ruthless honesty, it had ever made any difference to him at all what she thought. He had certainly never said anything about continuing their relationship, once these few weeks had passed. He had said only that it had been fun . . .

A shadow detached itself from the darkness under the big trees that rimmed the garden, and came up the steps to the terrace. She saw it out of the corner of her eye, and she didn't turn around. It was a shadow wearing evening clothes . . .

'Adam,' she said. Her voice shook a little.

'Sorry to disturb you.' He didn't pause. 'I hope you don't mind; I didn't want to walk all the way around to the front.'

'I need to talk to you.'

He didn't turn, but he stopped with his hand on the knob of the french door. 'Why now?' he asked reasonably. 'You haven't had much to say to me for the better part of a week.'

'I know,' she said miserably. 'And I'm sorry about that. I should have known that you wouldn't—that you couldn't——' She stopped, and tried again. 'You never had any intention of destroying Ashton Court, did you? Despite what you said to Phillip that day.'

He turned around then and leaned against the french door, his arms folded. 'Congratulations,' he mocked. 'You're finally catching on.'

The sarcasm stung. 'I can't help it that I've been confused, Adam.'

'No,' he said. 'I don't suppose you could. It was beyond you to believe that I might actually have had Olivia's best interests at heart, and not my own.'

'You have to admit, the whole thing looked odd.' She caught herself. This was, after all, supposed to be an abject apology. 'I'm very sorry,' she whispered. 'Can't we just leave it at that?'

For a moment she thought he hadn't heard, but then he nodded stiffly. 'I would appreciate it if you'd stay here with Olivia till she moves into her apartment,' he said.

She was confused. 'I thought——'

'Classes will be over next week.'

'I know, but I assumed you would be staying for a while at least.'

'Of course,' he said with bleak humour. 'That's why

you decided to move.'

There was no answering that; it was true, after all. 'What are you going to do?' she asked hesitantly.

'I told you once. I'll be in Chicago on the first day of September.' He sighed. 'After that, I don't know. Olivia will always know where to find me.'

'Are you going back to being a vagabond?'

'I don't know. I used to wander around so much because I was always searching. Perhaps I always will be.' He sounded a little bitter.

'Looking for your father?' she said softly, with a pang of understanding.

He shook his head. 'No. There's nothing to show me where to look, and I've already been luckier than I had any reason to expect.'

'I see.' But what had he meant, then? she wondered. 'I wish you well, Adam. Surely at least we can say goodbye on a friendly note.'

He shook his head. 'We've never been friends,' he said. 'Friends trust each other.'

She bit her tongue, and then something deep inside her splintered into raw pain, an agony that refused to listen calmly and be blamed for everything that had gone wrong between them. She said, feeling as if the words were being forced out of her, 'And friends tell each other the truth, Adam Merrill. You should have told me what you were doing!'

His eyes were blazing; the violet-blue had turned to almost black. 'Do you know why I didn't? Because it was important to me to have you trust me. I needed to know that you believed me without explanations——'

She flinched away from the bitterness in his voice, and put a hand up as if to defend herself.

'You couldn't do that, could you. Sara? You couldn't bring yourself to trust me.'

But I did, she thought. Deep down, I did believe in you. But my mind said one thing, and my heart another, and it tore me apart, not to *know*. And by the time I realised that I truly could put my faith in you, despite those doubts, it was too late—I'd destroyed everything, then.

'Did you really believe I could destroy this house? I could never live in it; it's not my kind of life at all, but to rip it down——' His voice was savage. 'Sara, how could you believe that I am capable of that?'

'It wasn't Ashton Court I meant at all,' she whispered.

He frowned, and said carefully, 'Then what in hell do you mean?'

She wet her lips and said softly, 'About Pamela. What you were searching for, and—and what you are——' She swallowed hard. 'If you cared about me, Adam, you should have told me!'

'You said that nothing mattered except what we ourselves were,' he reminded.

'And I believe that. But this is a part of you, a very important part of you. Don't you see, Adam? When I told you about Guy, it wasn't just because of who he was, but because the experience made me what I am. And——'

'And you've judged me over and over as if I was that two-timing fraud you used to worship. Dammit, Sara, I will not be put in a category with him!'

She was trembling, but she didn't even know if it was from the chill of the air or the sudden hope that had sprung to life inside her, like the tiniest flicker of a newly lit candle.

He scowled at her. 'That hurt, you know,' he accused. 'The night you welcomed me into your bed, I thought we had put all the questions about trust behind us. Do you really believe I could do that, Sara? Make love to you for no more reason than my own convenience?'

She remembered the way he had held her that night, and how he had been so careful to make certain that the pleasure of it belonged to both of them, and she was ashamed of herself for questioning his motives, for even the briefest second.

'No,' she said. 'But——'

'I wanted to tell you about Pamela,' he whispered. 'But I thought there would be plenty of time to share all the dead ends in my life, all the foolish things I've done.' He came slowly toward her across the terrace.

A tiny flicker of hope slid painfully along each nerve. Of course, she thought. How foolish I've been. He thought it was just another dead end; he would have told me if he'd had any idea it was going to explode under our very feet like that. You can have all the time in the world, my love, she wanted to say. All the time there is . . .

He stopped short a couple of feet from her.

'Adam——' Her voice cracked. She reached out, because she couldn't bear not to be touching him, and put her hand on his dark sleeve. 'About Guy—yes, I worshipped him.'

His arm tensed, and for a instant she thought he was going to shake her off like a troublesome insect and walk away.

'I adored him,' she went on softly. 'Or perhaps I should say I adored what I thought he was. It's different with you. I don't adore you, but I love you——'

He stared down at her, his eyes dark and steady.

'—for what you are,' she finished steadily. 'And the only thing I want is a chance to show you that I will trust you with my life.'

There was a long, breathless silence. 'The only thing?' he asked gravely, and for an instant fear tingled along her veins. Had she bared her soul for nothing? Was it too late, after all, to salvage what they might have been able to build? Then she saw the dancing light that had sprung into his eyes, and she flung herself against him with a little sob.

His arms tightened around her. 'Oh, God, I love you,' he said huskily, and then his mouth on hers drowned out the questions and the problems and the pain of the last week.

When he raised his head, her senses were swimming and she could scarcely stand up. She put a shaking hand up to her hair. He had run his fingers through it, and it was trailing down around her shoulders in disordered wisps. 'And once I actually thought you had too much experience at kissing to mess up a woman's hair,' she managed to whisper.

'I have only started to learn,' he said, and pulled her back against him. 'Come with me, Sara?'

'To Chicago?'

'More than that,' he said. 'I want you wherever I go.'

It sent a ripple of happiness to her heart, followed by a pang. 'I wish I could,' she said. 'But I can't just walk out on my job. It wouldn't be fair to Dave Talbot, and I'd have a dreadful time getting another position.'

He raised an eyebrow. 'You'll trust me with your life, hmm?' he quoted drily.

She closed her eyes in pain and leaned her forehead against his shoulder. It wasn't such a warm and comforting place to be, after all, she decided. She had a choice to make, and very little time to think about it . . .

Trust, she thought. It was such a sharp sword, sometimes, without a safe handle to grasp anywhere. She could have the safety of her job, or she could have Adam. She could have the warm nest of comfort that Chandler College had become for her, or she could take life as it came, by his side.

But there was no choice, not really. With him, life might be one crazy incident after another, but without him, there was no life at all.

'I'll go,' she said, before she could dwell on the risks. 'But you'll have to tell Dave Talbot, because I just can't——'

'Tell him what? Classes don't start till the second week of September. That's plenty of time for us to have a honeymoon, and me to start a new book, before we have to come back and get settled into an apartment somewhere not too far from Olivia.'

Sara gave a furious little scream. 'You could have told me that you would actually give up your case of wanderlust and stay here!'

'Well, I won't promise to be happy here for ever. But for a year or two——' He gave her a mischievous smile. 'Besides, I'm only protecting myself,' he murmured. 'Who knows when the market for trash is going to collapse and you'll have to support me?'

'It's good trash,' she said automatically. 'But I'll never forgive you for making me choose.'

'And I'll never forget the choice you made,' he said, suddenly serious, and kissed her again, and she promptly forgot what she'd been irritated about.

It was a long time later when they decided it was too cold to sit on the terrace any longer and went back inside. 'I'll have to get your aquamarine resized,' Adam was saying.

'Why? It fits.'

'On the wrong hand.' He held up her left hand and kissed the spot at the base of the third finger. 'This one's reserved for a different kind of ring.'

'Oh.' It was shy. 'You did say something about a honeymoon, didn't you?'

'Yes. I suppose this state has a waiting period for those wishing to commit matrimony?'

'Three days.'

'So if we get our licence on Monday, which is the earliest the courthouse will be open, we can be married on Thursday——'

'I can't possibly put together a wedding before Thursday,' Sara objected.

'What's to put together? Olivia can have the collar and cuffs finished on your new dress by then, and I'll bet I can line up a priest in nothing flat. It won't take my parents three days to fly out here. What else do we need?'

She frowned. 'Are you certain, Adam?'

'Aren't you? After all, you did propose to me a long time ago. And——' He stopped, tipped her chin up till she had to meet his eyes, and said very seriously, 'I'm sorry, my love. I am so very sure, you see, that I just don't see any reason to delay. But if you really aren't ready, Sara, we'll wait.'

She looked up at him, and all her doubts burned up in a sudden little blaze of happiness. He was right, she thought. What was there to wait for, when they could be together? 'Thursday,' she agreed.

Adam grinned. 'In that case, the biggest problem I can see is what we're going to do with ourselves every night till Thursday.'

The wicked suggestiveness in his voice sent tiny ripples of anticipation through her body. 'Mr Merrill,' she said, doing her best to sound shocked, 'are you making improper advances to a lady? And to consider that your father is a man of the cloth!'

'Who understands the weaknesses of human flesh, my dear. No, I can't see any help for it; we're just going to have to drop sleeping pills in Olivia's after-dinner coffee.'

'Don't bother,' a voice said calmly out of the darkest corner of the little den. 'I'm really a very sound sleeper, especially when I know that the people I love are happy.' Olivia gave Sara a warm hug and stood on her toes to kiss Adam's cheek. 'But I must admit you two have given me a few restless nights lately. Would you like to have some hot chocolate with me? No? I think I'll take mine up to my room, then. Goodnight, my dears.'

'I'll be damned,' Adam said, after the old lady had vanished up the stairs. He sounded as if someone had knocked all the breath out of him, but a moment later the teasing tone was in his voice again as he pulled Sara back into his arms. 'We'll have to do some rewriting of the vows, of course,' he said. 'You will agree to love, honour, and read my books—won't you?'

'As long as you don't put in anything about limericks.'

'I promise. Actually, for the last couple of weeks I've been wanting to write sonnets instead—but when I look at you the only thing I can think of is "How do I love thee? Let me count the ways——" '

The humour had died out of his voice.

'Sara, my love,' he whispered. 'My dear and only love——'

She put her head down on his shoulder. 'Keep counting,' she recommended. 'I've got the rest of my life to listen.'

IS PASSION A CRIME?

HOT ICE *by Nora Roberts* £2.9

A reckless, beautiful, wealthy woman and a professional thief. Red h
passion meets cold hard cash and it all adds up to a sizzling novel
romantic suspense.

GAMES *by Irma Walker* £2.5
(Best selling author of Airforce Wives under the name of Ruth Walker)

Tori Cockran is forced to save her son by the same means th
destroyed her marriage and her father – gambling. But first she mu
prove to the casino boss she loves that she's not a liar and a chea

SEASONS OF ENCHANTMENT *by Casey Douglas* £2.7

Ten years after their broken marriage and the loss of their baby, ca
Beth and Marsh risk a second chance at love? Or will their differenc
in background still be a barrier?

All available from February 1989.

W⦿RLDWIDE

From: Boots, Martins, John Menzies, W H Smith, Woolworths and
other paperback stockists.